P9-DEV-271

THE FUR FLIES

A dark form flew through the air, coming straight for the window.

Raider grabbed the girl and pushed her out of the way.

The animal crashed through the panes of glass, landing in the middle of the kitchen table. Raider lifted the Winchester and fired two shots into the creature. It fell, writhing on the floor. He shot it again, to make sure it was dead.

The girl began to scream.

Raider grabbed her and lifted her to her feet.

He could hear the others outside, circling the back porch. He fired through the window, scaring them back, shooting until the last cartridge was gone.

"We got to get out of here," he told the girl.

She nodded, holding his hand.

"Not through the back door," he said, kneeling. "Just climb on if you wanna stay alive."

She got onto his back.

Raider grabbed the oil lamp and dashed it against the wall of the house. The flames started to rise toward the ceiling. He knew the fire would keep them back, at least until he escaped through the front.

He stepped over the dead animal. It appeared to be a wolf, but he couldn't be sure. He had to run for now, to get away with his life . . .

Other books in the RAIDER series by
J. D. Hardin

RAIDER
SIXGUN CIRCUS
THE YUMA ROUNDUP
THE GUNS OF EL DORADO
THIRST FOR VENGEANCE
DEATH'S DEAL
VENGEANCE RIDE
CHEYENNE FRAUD
THE GULF PIRATES
TIMBER WAR
SILVER CITY AMBUSH
THE NORTHWEST RAILROAD WAR
THE MADMAN'S BLADE
WOLF CREEK FEUD
BAJA DIABLO
STAGECOACH RANSOM
RIVERBOAT GOLD
WILDERNESS MANHUNT
SINS OF THE GUNSLINGER
BLACK HILLS TRACKDOWN
GUNFIGHTER'S SHOWDOWN
THE ANDERSON VALLEY SHOOT-OUT
BADLANDS PATROL
THE YELLOWSTONE THIEVES
THE ARKANSAS HELLRIDER
BORDER WAR
THE EAST TEXAS DECEPTION
DEADLY AVENGERS
HIGHWAY OF DEATH
THE PINKERTON KILLERS
TOMBSTONE TERRITORY
MEXICAN SHOWDOWN
THE CALIFORNIA KID
BORDER LAW
HANGMAN'S LAW
FAST DEATH
DESERT DEATH TRAP
WYOMING AMBUSH

RAIDER

KILLER'S MOON

BERKLEY BOOKS, NEW YORK

KILLER'S MOON

A Berkley Book / published by arrangement with
the author

PRINTING HISTORY
Berkley edition / September 1990

All rights reserved.
Copyright © 1990 by The Berkley Publishing Group.
This book may not be reproduced in whole or in part, by
mimeograph or any other means, without permission.
For information address: The Berkley Publishing Group,
200 Madison Avenue, New York, New York 10016.

ISBN: 0-425-12271-9

A BERKLEY BOOK® TM 757,375
Berkley Books are published by The Berkley Publishing Group,
200 Madison Avenue, New York, New York 10016.
The name "BERKLEY" and the "B" logo
are trademarks belonging to Berkley Publishing Corporation.

PRINTED IN THE UNITED STATES OF AMERICA

10 9 8 7 6 5 4 3 2 1

This book is dedicated to Larry Feldman.

CHAPTER ONE

A hot, dusty, deep summer wind swept over Albuquerque, New Mexico, pushing Raider toward the edge of town. The tall, rough-hewn Pinkerton agent hadn't been in New Mexico for a while, so he wasn't sure what he would find on the outskirts of the mountainous settlement, but he shifted painfully in the saddle, figuring he would have to give a try, go that extra mile to find what a man needed after a long ride.

The noon sun was high overhead, forcing the Mexican citizens to their siestas, but there were enough men and women on the street to notice the big man who stared straight ahead with a trail-hardened scowl on his face. They whispered to themselves, speculating as to the possibility of trouble from the dust-covered rider.

Raider was dressed like any other saddle tramp. A dusty black Stetson sat on his thick black hair. He wore a faded cotton shirt, leather vest, well-worn jeans, and boots that were badly in need of polishing. His eyes were as black as the slits in a rattler's diamond irises, his face stubbled with trail-growth, and his moustache had grown too long. He needed a bath, a meal, some whiskey, a stable for the gray gelding underneath him, and a willing woman. He hoped to find it on the edge of town.

The spectators gaped from the shade of porches and the safety of windows. Raider just kept his eyes straight ahead.

Somebody ran ahead of him to the sheriff's office. Raider saw the door open and a lawman emerged into the heat.

The sheriff studied the sooty rider, wondering if he had seen Raider before. The boy who had run for the lawman stood behind him, peering up at the big man. The words formed on the sheriff's lips.

"He's the Pinkerton."

The sheriff gawked when Raider reined back on the gray. It had been a good animal so far, in spite of the way Raider had ridden it. They both deserved a rest, the big man thought.

Raider tipped back his Stetson and tried to smile at the lawman. "Howdo, sheriff. Remember me?"

The sheriff's hand was hanging close to a big Remington. "You caught somebody for me once, didn't you? They call you Ranger or somethin' like that."

"Raider."

"Raider." The sheriff eased his hand away from the butt of the pistol. "What brings you up this way?"

Raider saw the nervousness in his eyes. Lawmen didn't want Pinks around unless they had a load of dirty work. Raider had almost gotten used to the attitudes of local constables. But he still didn't care much for them.

Raider didn't answer the sheriff right away, so the lawman repeated the question. "I said, what brings you up this way?"

Raider sighed and stretched in the saddle. "What the hell you think brings me up this way?"

The sheriff had to think about it. "Probably chasin' somebody," he said finally.

"Man name o' Salley. Gorman Salley. Only he's called Fats most o' the time. S'posed to be a real porker."

The sheriff rubbed his chin. "No, ain't seen no fat drifters through here lately. How long you been chasin' him?"

"Too long."

He didn't want to fool with the lawman any longer. Then he noticed the young man peering around his protector. Raider reached into his pocket and took out a silver dollar.

"Here," he said, tossing it to the frightened lad. "If a fat man shows up, you come tell me."

The boy, who was not as scared now, picked up the dollar from the dirt. "Where you gonna be?"

Raider nodded toward the end of town. "Millie's; if she's still there."

The sheriff turned red-faced, but he replied, "Yeah, she's still there. You can bet on that!"

The big Pinkerton agent from Arkansas couldn't resist a little fun, so he said, "Hey, is Millie still diddlin' the head o' the citizen committee?"

"Paw!" the boy cried. "That's my paw!"

The sheriff shooed the lad toward home. "No need for that kind of language in front of the boy, Pinkerton."

"Sorry," Raider replied, "I keep forgettin' how you law boys always have t' look the other way. Hell, the town pays your wages, so you have t' dance t' the tune that's called for ya."

"You better not cause no trouble in my town, Pinkerton!"

Raider eased the gray gelding away from the red-faced, bug-eyed lawman.

"I mean it!" the sheriff called.

He had already forgotten the last piece of chicken-plucking that Raider had done for the good town of Albuquerque. Who the hell had Raider brought in back then? Some thief or killer?

These thoughts reminded him that he was still chasing a fugitive from justice, a fat man named Salley. His quarry had killed some, lied some, stolen some. Enough to make the territory of Arizona request the services of a Pinkerton agent to apprehend the lawless fat man.

Raider had never figured that a hog could run so far so fast. Salley was giving him a good chase. Fat Salley. Fats.

Raider had to catch him.

And so far it was going pretty badly.

As he approached the stable, he could hear the lonely ringing of the blacksmith's hammer. There was another livery in town, but

Raider preferred the one on the outskirts of Albuquerque. The stableman there really knew horses and he wasn't just out to make a buck. His place wasn't fancy, but he always took good care of Raider's mounts, not to mention his fine selection of animals. He never had more than two or three horses to sell, but they were always top-notch choices.

The man came away from the forge when he saw Raider. "Howdy. You lookin' to board your animal?"

Raider came out of the saddle, feeling the creaks and catches in his bones and muscles. "Mebbe lookin' t' trade," he offered. "Take care o' this ol' boy an' tell me if you got anythin' better."

The stableman nodded, studying the tall stranger. "Ain't you the Pinkerton who rides through here every year or two?"

Raider nodded. "I am that. How'd you know it was me?"

The man pointed to the grip of the Colt that rested in the holster on Raider's hip. "You got a redwood handle on that hogleg. I remembered it. That rifle, too." He nodded to the scabbard on the sling ring of the saddle. "Seventy-six Winchester. Don't see many of them around. Takes the big cartridge, does it?"

"Yep. It's done right by me."

Raider took the rifle out of the scabbard and then shouldered his saddle bags.

"They made it for the buffalo," the livery man offered. "Only by the time the gun was ready, the buffalo was gone."

Raider turned his black irises on the stableman. "Listen up. You seen a fat man through here? A stranger?"

"No. There was a stranger come through, may even still be in town. But he was a skinny man, like a reed."

"I want the best for that pony," Raider ordered. "He's been good to me an' now I wanna return the favor."

The livery man smiled and nodded appreciatively. "It's a great pleasure to see a man so concerned about his animal."

As Raider strode away from the stable, he thought of all the mounts he had ridden straight into the ground in pursuit of outlaws.

"Where you gonna be?" the man called after him.

"At Millie's!"

Raider headed for the yellow, two-story house that lay another quarter mile up the road. He wondered if Millie would be glad to see him. He couldn't remember exactly what had happened on his last visit to the yellow cathouse. He'd know if he was in trouble as soon as he saw the look on Millie's face.

The place seemed quiet as he clomped up the front steps. Millie always had clean girls and fresh bathwater. The front door was open, so he pushed in. Before he took three steps, he heard the woman's voice.

"Just what do you think you're doin', cowboy?"

Raider's heart sank. It was Millie raging at him. Her angry face almost turned him back to the door.

"Hey, it's me, honey," he offered politely with his arms outstretched.

She was still frowning. "Who the hell—"

It could be real nasty if she was holding a grudge against him.

Her face seemed to soften. "Raider?"

He nodded. "I'm 'fraid so."

"Raider!"

When she smiled, he knew everything was going to be all right. At least until he thought about chasing the fat man again.

CHAPTER TWO

Business was not as usual in the offices of the Pinkerton National Detective Agency. An atmosphere of gloom had fallen over the agency, due mainly to a tirade that was in progress in Allan Pinkerton's private sanctum. Henry Stokes, one of the agency's best operatives, was the recipient of a severe dressing-down that could be heard by the rest of the staff.

"Where do you get off blowing up a bridge?" Pinkerton ranted. "Do you have any idea what this will cost the agency if we have to pay for it?"

William Wagner cringed at his desk. He rubbed the lenses of his wire-rimmed spectacles with a clean handkerchief. Wagner, Pinkerton's assistant, feared what Stokes might do if the reprisal was too strident.

"A bridge!" Pinkerton cried.

Suddenly the voice of Henry Stokes resounded through the muggy summer air. "I stopped him, didn't I?"

Wagner winced, replacing his glasses on the bridge of his nose. Sweat stained his limp collar. He felt rumpled and useless in the heat. And now it seemed he was going to lose one of his best agents.

"Our policy," Pinkerton started, "is to—"

"I don't give two meadow wafers for your policy!" Henry Stokes cried. "You wanted that thief stopped, so I stopped him."

"If you value your job, Henry Stokes, you'll—"

That was the final straw, apparently. The door to Pinkerton's office flew open and Henry Stokes stormed toward the front entrance. Wagner sighed, glancing down at the letter on his desk. He had wanted Stokes for the assignment, but now that was going to be impossible, at least for a couple of weeks. It would take that long to talk Pinkerton into rehiring Stokes. And the quarrelsome agent would require some coaxing before he swallowed his pride and came back.

Pinkerton was right behind Stokes, wagging a finger in the air. "You won't be back this time, Stokes! Do you hear me?"

Henry slammed the front door behind him.

Pinkerton, nostrils flaring, eyes bulging, cast his frightful gaze around the office. "Back to work. All of you! And William"—glaring straight at the bespectacled man—"I don't want to be disturbed."

He slammed the door to his office.

A deathly silence settled in on the agency.

Wagner could not wait too long. The letter on his desk said that the matter was urgent. Still, there was no sense in approaching his boss until the big Scotsman had cooled down.

So Wagner waited for fifteen minutes and then tapped lightly at the door.

"Come in!"

Pinkerton was red-faced behind his big desk. "That Stokes! He'll not be employed by us again."

Wagner nodded. "Here. I thought you'd want to see this. It came in today by post. The man on the other end says he couldn't afford a telegram."

Pinkerton snatched the paper from Wagner's hand. Huffing a bit, he started to read the letter. Then the text began to sink in.

Pinkerton leaned back, forgetting the fight he had just finished with one of his agents.

"William," he said, stroking his beard, "this is serious. A bit farfetched, but still serious if there's any truth to it."

Wagner had to say the obvious. "I was considering Stokes for the job, but now—"

"Stokes! He blew up a bridge to catch that train thief. And we'll probably have to pay for it."

Wagner shrugged. "Maybe not. The state of Nebraska is awfully glad to be rid of that train robber."

Pinkerton ruminated, wiping the sweat from his brow with a wet cloth. "Stokes won't do this job, not now, not ever."

Wagner could not argue with that.

"Where's Raider?" Pinkerton asked.

"Arizona, the last I heard from him. Although he could be anywhere. He's after some local thief."

Pinkerton sighed. "Isn't he always?"

"Shall I pull him off the case and send him on this matter?" Wagner asked. "It does seem like the logical thing to do."

The burly Scotsman considered it for a moment before he nodded. "Yes, Raider is the man."

Wagner turned to go.

"And don't let Henry Stokes back in this office!" Pinkerton cried.

Wagner knew better, but he still held his tongue.

Back at his desk, Wagner started the procedure for finding one of his agents. He would send telegraph messages to any place that had a wire, a message for Pinkerton agents, asking if they had seen Raider. He would also send a wire in Raider's own name.

In the meantime, he thought, he could send somebody else to Texas to look into the matter.

Wagner read the letter again, shuddering. A cold chill ran over him, even in the heat of the day. Raider was the only one he could send, now that Stokes had quit.

It was an eerie case. Wagner didn't envy Raider one bit.

CHAPTER THREE

Millie lifted the bucket, pouring another gusher of cold water over Raider's black hair. "You're lucky," she said to the big man. "I don't usually let anyone use the tub this early in the day. But then again, you were always special, Raider."

The big man from Arkansas leaned back in the wooden tub, watching as Millie went to the pump for a bucketful of water. She had pretty much retired from whoring, but that fact seemed to be agreeable for her. Millie was shaped the way Raider liked them; big-chested and broad-beamed. Dark brown curls formed a corona around her head, framing an attractive, thick-lipped face. Now that he was clean, Raider began to feel the urge.

He held out the bar of fancy soap that she had given him. "Millie, how 'bout washin' my back?"

She hesitated at the pump, frowning at him. Her blue silk robe had fallen open a little. Raider could see the moist shadow of her bosom, skin as white as fine pearls.

Millie shook her head. "I ain't washin' your back."

"Aw, why not?"

"Because, " she replied, "I'll get to washin' your back and pretty soon you'll want me to wash your front."

Raider drew the soap back. "Aw, be that way."

She laughed a little. "Poutin' won't work either, Raider."

"I ain't poutin'!"

But he was and he knew it so he started to soap his own arms and chest.

Millie pumped the bucket full and carried it back toward the tub. "So, Raider, you still a Pinkerton?"

"Yeah, I'm a Pinkerton. One who needs his back washed."

Millie set the bucket next to the tub. "You never give up."

"I just been havin' a rough time of it on this one," he said. "This case I mean. Chasin' a fat boy. You ain't seen one through here lately, have you? Name's Salley, Gorman Salley. They call him Fats."

She shook her pretty head. "Don't tell me you can't catch a fat one," she teased. "They don't move very fast."

He sighed. "Well, I don't know, Millie. Yore ol' Arkansas grandaddy ain't what he once was."

She snatched the soap from his hands. "Dog it all, if you're gonna sound that pitiful, Raider, I might as well wash your back for you."

Her hands felt good on his shoulders. She massaged the muscles around his neck, working out the soreness. Raider was glad that she had a bathhouse in back of the brothel. It made things a lot easier for a dirt-eating trail rider. The smell of her perfume was a welcome diversion as well.

"That feels so good, Millie."

She didn't say anything, but kept washing his back and shoulders.

As she bent over him, her breasts brushed against the back of his head. Her nipples had grown rigid. Raider felt a stirring below, but he fought off the urge to grab her and pull her into the tub with him. Millie was bull-headed, so if she said she didn't want it, he was not going to push her.

"Yeah, this Salley is givin' me a fit," Raider went on. "I lost his trail in Flagstaff. He was headin' this way, though, so I hope I can find him this week."

Millie's hand strayed over his shoulder, down his chest.

Raider touched her fingers. "Hey, I thought you didn't wanna wash my front, honey."

He looked back to see the languid expression on her face. Her eyes were heavy, her mouth parted. She was staring into the tub.

Raider glanced down to see that his rigid member had broken the surface of the cool water. Millie was staring straight at it. Sweat dripped from the end of her nose.

"What're you lookin' at?" Raider teased.

Millie only knelt by the side of the tub. She had forgotten how big he was. It brought back memories of being in bed with him, years before, when she was still whoring.

"Millie?"

She reached for him, grabbing his cock, wrapping her fingers around the massive member.

Raider flinched. "Don't start somethin' you won't finish, lady."

She touched the bar of soap to his prick. Slowly, her hands began to work him up and down, raising a lather on his fleshy length. Raider leaned back, enjoying the attentions to his cock.

She was going to toss him off. He had done it himself countless times, but some fine lady's soft hand always felt a lot better. The soap didn't hurt any, either. His sap was rising just as Millie took her hand away.

"Hey," he protested, "I told you not to—"

Millie stood up, looking down at him with a lustful expression on her round face. "I ain't done it with a man for a long time, Raider, but I want to do it with you."

He smiled. "Hop on in this tub and have a sit down."

She knelt again, lowering her face, kissing him. Her tongue darted in and out of his mouth. He could feel her need, her hunger, like a mare that had been in the pen too long and wanted her freedom.

He reached for her breasts, cupping the nipples.

Millie stood up again. "No! I mean, not like this, not here. I want it, but I want it in my own bed. You remember where my room is?"

"No."

She winked. "Top of the stairs on the right. And don't shave. I want to feel that beard on me."

She started for the back stairs.

"Hey," Raider called, "who's gonna dry me off?"

"Do it yourself."

Millie disappeared up the stairwell.

Raider climbed out of the tub, reaching for a coarse towel. Why the hell hadn't she done it with him in the water? That would have been easiest. Then they wouldn't have had as far to walk to the kitchen, where he could rustle up a hot meal.

Of course, he was ready for bed. The swelling had only increased after she left him. Millie knew how to make a man want her and Raider surely had a yearning to get between her legs.

He wrapped the towel around himself, but it wouldn't hide his erection.

Millie had given his clothes to a Mexican woman who was scrubbing them in a wash tub so the towel had to do for now.

Raider picked up his rifle and his holster. He wasn't giving his guns to anyone. He never let them out of his sight. A Pink stayed alive a lot longer if he kept his iron at hand.

His feet left wet tracks as he stomped up the steps.

He couldn't remember which door belonged to Millie, but it didn't matter because the door to her room was open.

Millie lay back on the soft bed, her thick body completely naked.

Raider smiled and then he saw that she wasn't alone. A thin, dark-skinned young woman lay on the bed next to Millie. That was the way it went, Raider thought. One minute you didn't have any woman and the next minute you had two. Not a bad hand to play.

The big man sure as hell wasn't going to complain.

Raider leaned his rifle against the wall next to the bed. Then he hung his gun belt on the bedpost. He had to play it safe, even if he did have a hunch that the fat man was nowhere to be found in New Mexico. His first bust as a Pink. It had to happen sooner or later.

He gazed down at the two naked women who lay on the soft mattress. Millie was holding the other girl's hand. Millie stroked the back of her hand, like the girl was nervous.

"Your friend got a name?" Raider asked.

"Consuela," Millie replied. "She keeps me company at night. Only, well, she has to go to work, to earn her keep like everyone else. She's a mite skittish so—"

Raider's brow fretted. "So you thought you'd let me break her in."

Millie grinned. "Well, you do know the ways of women, Raider."

"I ain't bustin' no cherries, Millie. You know how I am 'bout that. I ain't never been much on virgins."

The dark-skinned girl leaned up on one arm, glaring at him. "I am no virgin. I have had men. I hate them."

She planted a kiss on Millie's thick lips.

Millie pushed her back. "Now, honey, let Raider show you a few tricks. He'll make you feel—well, like a bell ringing inside you."

Consuela leaned back on the mattress. "Never."

Raider had seen it before with women who whored. They stopped liking men and took up with their own kind. Somehow it seemed almost natural to the big man, though it made him sick when members of his own gender did the same sort of thing.

His thighs rested against the bed. Millie reached for the towel, pulling it away from his torso. The dark-skinned girl gasped when she saw the turgid length between Raider's legs. She shuddered a little. Millie wrapped her arms around Consuela and told her not to be afraid.

Raider slid down on the mattress next to Millie. He no longer cared about the girl and her problems. He just wanted to ease the aching in his pulsing crotch.

Millie shivered when he kissed her shoulder. "Now watch us, Consuela. Like this. Um, cowboy, that feels good. You see, johns want it to seem like you really want them. And sometimes you do."

Raider's lips closed around the nipple of her breast. Millie sighed. She really wanted it this time. Lying with the girl had made her forget the pleasures of a ready man.

He put his hand between her legs.

Millie was wet.

He fingered the entrance of her cunt. She gasped, throwing her head back. All the time the other woman was watching.

Raider wondered how long it would take her to get going.

She grabbed his shoulders. "Put it in."

"Millie!" Consuela cried. "I thought you loved me!"

"I do, honey, but right now I want Raider to fuck the hell out of me."

What could he do but obey her wishes? Raider rolled into the notch between her legs. His prickhead prodded the moist crevices, sinking in when Millie thrust her hips upward. She was breathing like a well-run filly. Her fingernails dug deep into his ass.

"Hard," she told him. "As hard as you can."

Raider started to move. He collapsed on top of her, driving his cock in and out.

Millie shook, holding on for the ride, her face contorted in an expression of pleasant anguish.

The girl just watched them, frowning, but ever more enthralled by the bedroom spectacle.

Raider felt his sap rising.

Millie sensed the expansion inside her. "Don't do it. Pull out. I don't need no—"

She yelped when he withdrew, resting the tip of his cock on her stomach, flooding her skin with a thick liquid.

Millie reached down to touch it with her fingers. "See, that's the way you keep from getting in the family way, Consuela. Make him pull it out. Raider's the best."

He rolled off her, snuggling into the clean sheets. "I need some shut-eye, Millie."

"I thought you were going to teach Consuela!"

He didn't have to wait long for sleep to overtake him.

And when he finally woke up, the girls were back, with their sweet, naked surprises.

Someone had a hand on his prick. He was growing hard again. He heard Millie instructing the girl.

"See, that's right, touch it gentle-like at first, then when he starts to bulge, yank on it."

At first, the girl wasn't too adept. But then she seemed to catch on. Her hand moved quicker, up and down his length.

Raider opened his eyes, staring at Consuela. She was a beautiful woman with long, thick hair and flawless skin. His body suddenly craved the Spanish lady who pulled on his glans.

"Do him right," Millie said. "If he—"

Raider decided to take over. "That's okay, Millie. Why don't you leave me and Connie alone for a spell?" He smiled at her.

Millie winked and tiptoed toward the door. "Connie; I like that. From now on, she's Connie."

The girl gaped at her lover. "Millie—"

Raider turned her face toward him. "Honey, don't worry. I ain't gonna hurt you. An' any time you wanna stop, just say the word."

She looked at the floor. "I want to do it."

"Are you sure?"

She nodded.

Raider patted the mattress. "Then lay down here an' let me take a good look at you."

She reclined next to him on the bed.

"You're beautiful," he told her.

Her big black eyes turned up to him. She seemed so damned innocent. Raider shook his head. He just couldn't do it.

"Get on outta here, girl."

Consuela frowned. "What?"

"Just go. I cain't do it. Tell Millie t' come back in here." He started to roll off the bed.

The girl reached around and grabbed his cock. "No," she said. "I want it. I want it inside me."

He turned back to say no, but he saw that she had spread her legs. He found himself touching the thick tuft of black hair between her thighs. Then he dipped into the moistness there. She flinched when he found the right spot at the top of her cunt. She hadn't expected Raider to know about that.

"Just lie back," he told her. "It'll be all right."

She closed her eyes and grabbed a pillow with two hands.

Raider massaged her, watching as she lost control. He even licked her some, just because he couldn't resist her beauty. She was ready then. And he knew how he wanted her to take it.

"You get on top," he said. "Go on."

He helped her into position. She straddled him, guiding his prick to the folds of her vagina. She hesitated, her face slack, mouth open.

"Slow," he told her. "An' you can stop if it hurts."

But it didn't hurt.

Consuela smiled when he was all the way inside her. She began to work her hips, doing what felt good. Raider finally couldn't stand it anymore, so he turned her around and got on top. She liked that even more.

He pulled out at the moment of climax.

Consuela touched the milky discharge with her fingers. "Just like Millie," she said softly.

Raider touched her cheek. "You did good, honey. But don't worry, I won't say a thing to Millie."

Consuela looked at the ceiling. "No, I want to work. It's right."

Raider rolled off her and settled into the mattress again.

Before long, Millie had joined them. "How'd it go?" she asked.

Raider just grunted. He wanted to sleep again. But now the females were yapping. He still managed to drift in and out of slumber.

In his waking dreams, he saw a fat man in the distance, heading swiftly toward the sun-stained horizon, getting farther and farther away from the slow-moving gray gelding with the Pinkerton agent in the saddle.

CHAPTER FOUR

Things didn't seem so bad when Raider finally stirred back to life. It was dark outside and the party had begun at Millie's: probably a Saturday night wingding with drunk cowboys and townsmen who had an itch for the ladies. He perched on the edge of the bed, remembering that he was chasing a man named Fats.

His mind clicked down the list of things that had to be done if he was going to get back on the trail: Check at the livery, maybe trade for a new horse. Swing in a wide circle around the area. Maybe put up a few notices.

He decided against a wire to the home office, because Wagner might pull him off the case. Then the runty little man with eyeglasses would be able to say that Raider had finally failed for the first time. What a joke that would be in the agency!

He had to find Fats Salley. The wide circle might do it, but what if Salley had come through Albuquerque at night? He could have watered his horse and stolen enough grub without anyone ever seeing him. He might still be heading east, but for where? Raton, maybe, or further: Texas and beyond. Damn it all, how could a fat man hide so easily?

He climbed off the bed and fumbled in the shadows until he found the oil lamp. When the orange light filled the room, he saw his clothes on the chair, all cleaned and pressed. His Stetson had been dusted as well and his boots had been polished. Millie sure knew how to make a man feel welcome.

Raider tensed, grabbing a stitch in his side. Sore body. Getting old. Something didn't feel right as he pulled on his clean pants. Then the pain went away.

Raider decided to find Millie to ask her if she had a soap and razor. But she was way ahead of him. The razor lay next to a bowl and pitcher on a dresser across the room. A mirror hung on the wall above the dresser.

"I hope she has a brush," he said aloud.

Sure enough, the brush was in the bottom of the bowl. Raider poured some water and started to work up a lather. He looked at his face in the mirror. It startled him for a second when his own image loomed out at him. But then he lost interest and concentrated on lathering his beard.

The razor was a little dull, so he stropped it on the back of his holster.

He was brushing his beard again when the knock came on the door.

Raider tensed, reaching for his Colt immediately. "Yeah?"

A man's voice prompted him to thumb back the hammer of the revolver.

"Are you the Pinkerton?"

He pointed the barrel of the Colt at the door. "Who wants to know?"

Hesitation. Maybe there was a fat man on the other side of the door. A dead fat man if he tried anything stupid.

"Got a message from the telegraph office," the man finally said.

Raider didn't think that sounded right. "A wire message? This late?"

"The key operator lives at the office," the man replied quickly, "so he gets messages at all hours. They know he's there, so they send it on down the line."

Raider figured that was logical. He had seen it before. But he still wasn't convinced.

"Aw right, there's a message. Who's it from?"

"From a man name of Wagner. He's from the Pinkerton Agency. The sheriff said you was here."

Might as well take a chance, the big man thought. See what Wagner had to say. But he would keep the Colt pointed at the door.

"Come on in, slow-like," he said.

The door opened and a skinny man stepped into the room, gawking at the gun.

Raider sighed and lowered the Colt. No fat man here. He holstered the Colt and turned back to the mirror.

"What's it say?"

"Pardon?" the man said.

"The message."

A pause. "You got to stop chasin' this Gorman Salley and go to Texas."

Raider shook his head. "I ain't goin' nowhere till I have the fat man in ropes."

A deep rasp escaped from the man's lips. "I wish you hadn't said that, Pinkerton."

Raider heard the clicking of a pistol hammer.

He spun to look at the reed-thin little weasel. "Why the hell are you drawin' down on me?"

"I'm Gorman Salley."

Raider chortled. "You ain't fat."

"Heat dripped it out of me," Salley said, grinning. "And I knowed you was after me, so I couldn't eat. Have a nervous stomach. Barely keep anythin' down when I do eat."

The fat man had disappeared. Why couldn't Raider see it before? He stared down the bore of a derringer in Salley's hand.

"I thought I'd lose you," the outlaw went on. "But you were too good. How the hell were you trackin' me anyway?"

Raider shrugged. "Instinct, I reckon. You didn't leave me much."

Salley lifted the derringer. "Well, looks like I done kilt me a Pinkerton. So long, boy."

"Whoa," Raider said. "Let me know one thing, Gorman."

The outlaw frowned. "Like what?"

"How'd you get the message from the telegraph office?"

Salley shrugged. "Saw the key operator give it to a young boy. But the boy said you had give him a dollar to bring the message, so he thought he should do it right away. I said I was a friend of yourn and that I would take it to you. Had to give him another dollar."

As he talked, Raider lowered his hand toward the bowl and pitcher. He wanted to knock it at Salley. Give himself a chance to lunge for the Colt.

"You were smart, Gorman. And I never woulda found you, not lookin' the way you do. You took a chance comin' here t' kill me."

"I was worried you'd find me," the outlaw offered, "but I found you instead. Good-bye, Pinkerton."

Raider was going to launch the bowl, but then Millie came in behind the skinny rat. When his eyes shifted and he gave a half turn, Raider was able to reach for his gun.

Millie screamed.

Raider took aim.

Salley gawked at the bore of the Colt.

"Drop it," the big man cried.

But Consuela was right behind Millie. She stepped into the room, straight between Raider and the outlaw. All Salley had to do was wrap his arm around the girl's throat. Then he stuck the derringer to her forehead.

"She dies if I do."

Raider froze with the Colt in his hand.

Salley backed out of the room, using the girl as a shield.

Millie started after them until Raider grabbed her.

"No."

"But—"

He pulled her against the wall. "Hold still. Let him get on the stairs."

"Then what?"

"Then I'm goin' out the window," the big man replied.

As soon as he heard the clomping boots on the stairs, Raider moved toward the casement. The window was open in the heat, so he had no trouble stepping out onto the roof of the connecting bathhouse. He could hear Salley as he made his way through the kitchen.

Why the hell had the girl come in when she did?

Raider was just starting to like her and now she was going to die. Gorman Salley came out the back door, pulling Consuela with him.

"Salley!" Raider fired a shot at his feet.

Salley screeched and looked over his shoulder.

Consuela managed to wriggle out of the skinny man's grasp.

Salley pointed the derringer at Raider, but the big man knew he wouldn't be accurate with the small weapon. Still, Salley was shooting at him, and a dead man was a lot easier to bring back than a live one. The Colt streamed fire in the night.

Salley buckled when the slug tore through his forehead. He staggered backward, falling into the dust. Raider almost felt bad about cheating the hangman. But it couldn't be helped. The fat man was really gone now. The skinny body finally stopped twitching. Raider wondered if the territory of Arizona wanted Salley's remains.

He stepped back into the room.

Millie was right there. "Raider!"

He waved the barrel of the Colt. "It ain't nothin'. Just a visit from that boy I was chasin'. But he ain't gonna be stayin' for dinner."

She went to the window and gazed down at the corpse. "I thought you were chasin' a fat man."

"I was. But he ain't fat no more. Knew I was chasin' him. Tried t' come after me. He paid for it."

Millie pulled away from the window and started down the stairs. "Consuela is out there somewhere."

Raider was right behind her.

The cathouse was starting to empty out. Spectators, assured that the threat had passed, were piling into the yard. They circled the body, jockeying for a good vantage point. Several of them carried torches and oil lamps.

"Right in the head," somebody muttered.

A couple of them turned away to vomit.

Raider pushed through the crowd, gazing down at the slender bulk. "Damn." He knew he had to go through the man's pockets, to find out for sure if he was Gorman Salley, but suddenly the sheriff was there, bending over the body.

"You kill him?" the sheriff demanded of Raider.

The big man nodded. "That's the one I was chasin'."

The lawman frowned. "He ain't fat."

Raider chortled. "Sheriff, you better button your fly."

Everyone laughed.

Raider bent down, going through Salley's pockets. He came up with a letter addressed to Salley and a wanted poster on the same man. The sheriff surveyed the papers in the torchlight.

"It's him all right," the lawman said.

"Trail baked all the lard off him," Raider rejoined, "but it's the same man. He pretended he was a messenger, bringin' me a telegram. Tried to get the drop on me."

The sheriff started to put the evidence in his pocket.

"I need that," Raider said.

The sheriff grimaced. "For what?"

"Evidence. I gotta let the territory of Arizona know that this man is dead. I have t' search his mount, too. I'm bettin' it's somewhere hereabouts."

Reluctantly, the lawman gave Raider the papers. "Just get him the hell out of here, Pinkerton."

Raider tried to smile. "Sheriff, I was kinda hopin' you'd bury him. I mean, I'd be willin' t' pay ten dollars."

Before the lawman could reply, a man stepped forward. "I'll bury him for ten dollars."

"And who might you be?" Raider asked.

"The undertaker."

One of Millie's whores screamed and ran into the house.

"Guess she didn't like sleepin' with a gravedigger," Raider said.

"Ten dollars," the undertaker demanded.

He looked at the sheriff. "Okay by the law boy here?"

"Just get him in the ground," the sheriff replied. "And Pinkerton, I don't want you here come mornin'."

"I won't be," replied the tall agent. "I sure as hell won't be."

• • •

The cathouse was calm after the undertaker removed the body. Raider returned to Millie's room, where he found her with Consuela. They had their arms around each other. Their lips were touching, tongues mingling. They gazed toward Raider when he barged in on them.

"Sorry," the big man said, actually blushing, "I didn't know you two was here."

He started to ease out of the bedroom.

"No!" Consuela had said it. She was smiling.

Raider squinted at her. "Why are you so happy, girl?"

"I feel alive. The excitement. It made me afraid at first, but now I am happy."

He nodded to Millie. "She's makin' you that way."

He didn't feel right with both of them there.

"Raider?"

It was Millie this time.

Her knowing smile made him weak. "Raider, don't you want to get some sleep? You should be tired."

He wasn't tired. In fact, the blood was coursing through him at a rapid pace. The erection appeared out of nowhere. They both looked so damned pretty. And he had already known them, that very day. So why did it seem sinful with the three of them?

"Come on," Millie said. "Let us give you the royal treatment."

He didn't have to consider it for very long. "Why the hell not."

They undressed him, washed his body with cool water and a soft cloth, rubbed his aching muscles, kissed him, fondled him.

Millie surprised him by taking his cock into her mouth.

Consuela grimaced. "Ooh, that's awful."

Millie smiled at her. "Men will pay extra for the French way. If you learn it, we can make a lot more money. Here, try it."

With some coaxing from Millie, the girl finally took him in.

"Don't suck," Millie told her. "Just run your mouth along the edges. Look at him, he's your prisoner."

Raider wanted both of them at the same time. He pulled away from Consuela, slapping Millie lightly on her big rump. "Let's show her somethin' else."

Millie seemed to know what he wanted. She got down on all fours. Raider positioned himself behind her.

"Like dogs," Consuela cried, making a face, but then she saw that Millie was liking it.

Raider plowed her from behind, bouncing off her ass. When he came, he pulled out and shot all over her back.

"I want to try it," Consuela said.

Raider collapsed on the bed. He felt himself slipping away. The girl would have to wait. He knew there'd be a lot of things to take care of in the morning, but he had already decided to forget everything and have a good night's sleep.

CHAPTER FIVE

William Wagner stood across the street from the eroded storefront, watching the doorway. He hoped to find Henry Stokes at this address, as the former agent was known to frequent a rooming establishment upstairs. Sure enough, the rotund, harmless-looking detective emerged from the door at the height of midday, carrying a beer pitcher in his right hand.

Wagner crossed the street and fell in beside him. "Drinking so early, Henry?"

Stokes didn't even look at him. "Figured you'd be around sooner or later, Wagner."

"I need your services."

Stokes spat into the street. "That's for the old man. And tell him twice if you want to."

"Henry, what will you do? You've been working for me almost ten years. Only Raider has been at it longer than you."

Stokes chortled derisively. "Yeah? How is the old war-horse?"

"I haven't been able to find him just yet. That's why I need you, Henry. If I can square it with Pinkerton, will you come back?"

"I'm gonna be a copper," Henry offered. "A boy in blue."

Wagner laughed. "You? A policeman? You hate constables. Something else you have in common with Raider."

"Forget it, Wagner. I'm gonna go get my beer."

Wagner let him go. He knew Stokes was flush, having collected almost two months of back pay. But he would be looking for his job again when he had run out of funds.

When Wagner returned to the offices of the Pinkerton National Detective Agency, he found a fresh telegram on his desk.

It was from Raider.

CAUGHT GORMAN SALLEY. ARIZONA DON'T WANT HIM BACK. YOU REALLY WANT ME TO GO TO ODESSA, TEXAS?

"Of course I do," Wagner said to himself.

He called one of the clerks and told him to take the message to the telegraph office.

Pinkerton came out when he heard the commotion. "What is it, William? Is the place on fire?"

"I heard from Raider," Wagner replied.

"Might as well be on fire," Pinkerton said. "Do we have to replace him on his current case?"

"No, he wrapped it up. Only—"

Pinkerton glared a his second in command. "Don't be tongue-tied, William. Come right out and say it."

"Well, he sent another telegram, asking me to confirm the first one I sent him."

Pinkerton nodded. "Smart of him, the big lummox. He's finally starting to follow procedure."

Raider probably just wanted another day off, Wagner thought, although he kept it to himself.

"I'm sending him to Texas," he replied instead. "We shouldn't wait too much longer on that one."

Pinkerton frowned, rubbing his chin. "It's not Texas that worries me. I want to know who we're going to send to Carson City."

Wagner sighed. He knew the perfect man. Henry Stokes. But Stokes no longer accepted wages from the agency.

Pinkerton seemed to be reading his assistant's mind. "Do you think you can get him back, William?"

Wagner wanted to stretch his boss's patience, since Pinkerton had been the one to drive the agent away in the first place. "Get *who* back, sir?"

Pinkerton turned red. "Henry Stokes! You know darned well who I mean, William. He's perfect for the case in Carson City."

Wagner shrugged. "The last I heard, Stokes had intentions of becoming a constable on patrol."

Pinkerton bellowed. "Stokes, a copper? Hah! He'd never make it. And if he tries, well, I'll just use my influence at the police station. They'll never take him on."

"He'll be ready to come back when he's broke," Wagner offered. "Until then, I'll send Avery to Carson City."

"Make sure you find a way of telling Stokes that Avery took a case meant for him. That should make him envious."

Wagner agreed that it would.

Pinkerton returned to his office.

Wagner took a deep breath. He didn't want to send Avery to Nevada, but he had to; at least until Stokes got tired of drinking beer and wanted his old job. Too bad he couldn't send Raider to both places.

But the big man from Arkansas was heading for Texas.

Maybe the hillbilly Pinkerton would meet his match in Odessa.

Or something close.

CHAPTER SIX

Raider was sleeping between Consuela and Millie when Wagner's telegram arrived. The sheriff brought it in person. Raider had ignored the lawman's directive to get out of town but the constable hadn't pressed the issue. As long as Raider stayed in Millie's cathouse and out of trouble, nobody was going to run him out of town.

He made the sheriff wait downstairs while he dressed. It was the first time he had worn clothes in two days. The girls were keeping him busy. It was making him start to feel sort of wicked and sinful. He needed to get back to work before something bad happened.

The sheriff was pacing in the main parlor. "Sorry to bother you," he quipped sarcastically.

Raider laughed. "Yeah, like you ain't never come here yourself."

The lawman grew red-faced, but he didn't say much else.

Raider took the telegraph message and read it. Odessa, Texas, it was. Report to a man named Jubal Chaney. Urgent.

He chortled. Weren't they all urgent? Wasn't everybody who hired him in desperate need of his services? People always thought their particular troubles were the worst—and usually they were; at least by the time they got around to calling Raider in.

"I reckon this means you'll be leaving," the sheriff said.

Raider grimaced at the lawman. "Yeah, you can rest easy. I'll be on my way, hoss. You'll be rid of me."

"That's not what I meant, Raider. I—well, I was wondering if you could help me with a problem."

Raider shook his head, grinning like a possum stealing persimmons. A chance to have some fun. Maybe show up the law boy.

"I knowed it'd come t' this sooner or later," he said disgustedly. "You always want a favor."

The sheriff lowered his head. "I reckon I had that comin'. The truth is, I envy you Pinkertons. And I'm only comin' to you with this because, well, my wife is involved."

That sounded more interesting to the big man. Maybe she was cheating on her husband or had a plan to give him the ax in the head at four in the morning. Women could always get you while you were sleeping.

But it was nothing that steamy.

"It's her jewelry," the sheriff went on. "Somebody's been stealing it right off her night table. She thinks I'm taking it, but I'm not. I can't figure out who's doing it. I sat watch all day for a couple of weeks and I ain't seen a thing."

"Ever think about night watch?" the big man said in a challenging tone. "That's when the thief is gettin' you."

The sheriff frowned. "But we're sleepin' right there. I'm a light sleeper too. I'd wake up if anybody came in."

Raider waved him off. "Listen, I could waste time explainin', but I want to get outta here. I'll see you after dark."

"Just like that," the lawman said, his hands extended.

"Pretty much."

"And you think you can catch the thief."

Raider shrugged. "I know I can."

"You're pretty cocky."

"Yep."

The sheriff finally turned away and started for the door.

"One more thing," Raider said.

"Yeah?"

"I need some things."

"Anything," the lawman offered.

"Some stinky cheese," Raider replied.

"What?"

"An' a house cat."

The sheriff gawked at him. "The hell you say."

"Just get it," Raider said, "an' I'll stop your thief."

There were a few tasks that awaited him before he left town. He had to go to the telegraph office and wire his confirmation to Wagner. Then he would try to make a trade at the livery. Raider could have taken stagecoaches and rail cars to Odessa, but he always preferred a trail ride. He knew the back paths and shortcuts, the different passes where time could be saved on a long ride. Albuquerque to Odessa—he could make it in a week if he hurried, ten days if he didn't.

But first he had to get out of the cathouse.

Consuela had taken a liking to him, a fact that now seemed to perturb Millie. They were sharing the dark-skinned woman and Raider could feel the tension building. Best just to forge straight ahead in the odds of the female cyclone.

They were still in bed when he returned to the sex-scented chamber.

"What did the sheriff want?" Millie asked.

Raider reached for his rifle and his holster. "I gotta go."

"No!" Consuela whined.

"It's okay," Millie intoned. "Go on, Raider."

She was glad to see him leave so she could have her plaything back.

Consuela stretched out her arms to Raider. "Kiss me goodbye."

He did it just to be polite.

Millie slapped his arm. "Get the hell out of here."

Consuela sulked beside her mistress.

Raider picked up his saddlebags and threw them over his shoulder. When his dusted Stetson was in place, he left the bedroom without looking back. Burning another bridge. He had come between Millie and the girl, so Millie wouldn't be happy to see him for a while. Maybe she'd get over it. Women could be forgiving if you stayed away long enough for them to forget.

He strode the quarter mile to the livery.

The stable man had been working on the gray. He said that he didn't have any better horses. Even though the gray was a sorry sight, it was still strong and ready. Good hocks and clean hooves.

So Raider saddled up and rode into town.

He stopped at the wire office first. The message went north to Wagner. There was also some back pay waiting for him. He decided to send a few bucks to Millie. That wouldn't square things with her, but it might take the sting out of the wound.

With some time to kill before dark, he went to the nearest saloon and ordered a mug of beer. Sitting at a table, he began to sift through his saddlebags, deciding on things he might need. When the inventory was completed, he left the saloon and went to the general store.

The clerk filled his list: cartridges for his rifle and his pistol, dried meat, a new cotton shirt, two pairs of socks, some oats for his pony, a tin mug that he would lose almost immediately, a new canteen, two cans of peaches, and a whetstone for his hunting knife.

Darkness still had not fallen on the mountain city, so he returned to the saloon for another mug of beer. He sat there, thinking of the women and his chances of burning in hell for the things he had done to them. Then the sheriff walked in and spoiled his daydream.

It was time to get back to work.

They sat in wooden chairs outside the sheriff's bedroom. The lawman had sent his wife away to her sister's house. He hadn't even let Raider get a good look at her: protecting his spouse. Raider couldn't blame him.

The sheriff shifted nervously in his chair. "I don't see what good this is doing."

Raider just sat there, listening. Next to his feet, resting on the floor, was a covered wicker basket that held a black-and-white house cat. Raider kept his ear on the door, anticipating the first disturbances of the thief.

"Are you loco?" the sheriff said.

Raider scowled at the lawman and pointed a finger. "You wanna finish this thing yourself?"

The sheriff backed off.

Raider looked down at the cat. "Well, Tom, it's 'bout time. I think we waited long enough."

He opened the basket and took out the cat.

"Are you sure the room is locked up tight, sheriff? I don't want puss here gettin' out."

The lawman nodded. "I still can't see—"

Raider opened the door and put the cat in the bedroom.

Somewhere in the house a clock struck ten.

It was almost midnight before anything happened.

Raider and the sheriff were sitting quietly when the commotion rose from the bedroom.

The lawman started to reach for the doorknob. "It's him."

Raider stopped him. "No, let Tom do the work for us."

There were sounds of debris falling on the floor, scuffling, a cat's howl, and squeaking that was barely audible.

Raider opened the door. "Here he comes."

Tom ran out with a rat in his mouth.

The sheriff gawked at the dead rodent. "What the hell—"

"Pack rat," Raider said. "Probably got a den somewhere nearby. Been sneakin' in at night and takin' your wife's stuff. If you find his den, you'll find the goods."

"I don't believe it."

"Believe it."

The clock struck twelve.

Raider rose out of the chair. "Well, sheriff, I reckon I done caught the thief for ya. I got real work t' do now."

The law boy was still shaking his head. "A consarned pack rat. I should have seen it."

"Yep, you should have."

Raider didn't wait for a reply. The gray was saddled and tied behind the sheriff's house. It was time to put his back to Albuquerque.

When he mounted up, he turned for a second to stare in the

direction of Millie's cathouse. He thought about the two women, perfumed and moist, rubbing against him. It hurt to urge the gray in a different direction but he started east, toward Texas.

The moon was high and bright against a clear sky, lighting his lonely way.

William Wagner hadn't expected two good things to happen in one day.

The telegraph message came from Raider, saying that the big man from Arkansas was on his way to Texas.

That left only one pressing matter; the incident in Nevada. Some gold missing from the U.S. Mint in Carson City. And so far, Avery hadn't even arrived in Nevada. What the hell had delayed him?

As Wagner pored over his papers, it took him some time to realize that there was a man standing quietly in front of his desk.

He looked up at a sheepish Henry Stokes. "You!"

"Okay," Stokes said.

Wagner leaned back in his chair. "Run out of money so soon, eh? Must've found a card game."

"Hey, I'm back, just like you asked, Wagner. Now if the old man wants to say he's sorry—"

At that very moment, as if prompted by the tone of Henry's voice, Allan Pinkerton came out of his office. "You!" he cried.

"Yeah," Stokes said, "Wagner begged me to come back, so here I am."

Pinkerton pointed toward the door. "You have work to do in Nevada, Mr. Stokes!"

With that, the head man slammed his door.

Stokes shrugged. "I reckon that'll have to do for an apology. Now, where was it you wanted me to go?"

Wagner gladly began to give him the details.

The sun was hot during the middle of the day, but Raider managed to avoid sunstroke by sleeping in the shadows. The mountains always provided plenty of shade and cool breezes. Even when he came down onto the broken mesas, he managed to stay hidden in the heat. The plains of southern New Mexico could be brutal in the summer, but Raider knew most of the tricks for staying alive.

Day sleeping and hard riding kept him confused. He lost track of the days, not sure how long he had been in the saddle. He shot small game for his meat, whenever he could find enough ground wood and twigs to make a fire. The dried beef kept him going in the absence of firewood.

Raider loved the plain in a strange way. It purified a man to sweat, to fear for his life, to deliver himself from the wilderness. Towns and cities brought out the worst in a man, catered to his weaknesses: gambling, whiskey, and women. But the plain made a man strong, sweated the evil out of him, wiped away his sins.

When he was a kid, forced by his uncle to listen to Sunday sermons, Raider had been afraid of hellfire talk, but he had grown out of that. And when he tried to consider Hell, he figured it couldn't be any worse than some of the places he had seen in his travels. If there was an afterlife, with a merciful God in charge, He surely wouldn't send anyone to the fires of Hell. Nobody could be that cruel; not after a man had been through a life on earth.

Raider stood on a windy mesa, feeling the soft breeze from the south. It was hot. He had his shirt off, facing west, watching as the sun descended behind the mountains. The big man felt like an Indian. He knew his spirit was fresh and clean, his sins erased. He enjoyed the moment of solace. Then he started down off the mesa, leading the gray gelding, picking up the trail for Odessa.

The ground leveled off and for a while Raider wasn't sure he was going to make it. There was no shade, except that provided by the gelding. Raider took off his Stetson and covered the animal's head. Then he hunkered for a few moments in the shade of the gelding's body.

They both had a drink from the canteen. Then Raider led the animal forward. He covered his own head with his shirt, tying it around his skull. The ground was a frying pan under his feet and Raider was dancing like water on a griddle. When his hopes were lowest, some clouds blew up from the south, covering the sun for a while.

Raider stopped to rest in the shade of a low canyon that suddenly appeared. When he ascended again, heading east, he saw the mountains in the distance. He had to make sure they weren't a mirage. If they were real, then they had to be the Guadalupe Mountains, and that meant he was close to the Texas border.

The clouds continued to build overhead. The air turned cooler. Raider swung into the saddle and drove hard toward the rising storm. Rain was rare in this section of the borderland. The droplets fell quickly from the sky, drenching the arid country. The gray held steady through the storm. Raider figured the animal wanted to be off the plain just as much as he did.

Raider reached the mountains by nightfall, officially crossing into the panhandle of Texas. The moon lighted the trail and Raider figured he would ride through the night, until he heard the music.

It was a mouth-harp, a harmonica, lilting through the cool mountain air. The tones lured him to the fire that rose in the half-darkness. A stranger sat by the fire, playing the instrument.

He turned when he saw Raider coming.

The man instantly stood up, like he was afraid. "Take anythin' I got, mister, just don't hurt me."

Raider waved him down. "Don't fret, pardner. I just wanted t' sit by your fire for a second."

The man seemed to take him at his word.

Raider dismounted and stretched before he hunkered by the fire.

"Couldn't find much wood," the man offered.

He noticed the stranger didn't have a mount. "You walkin' out here?"

"I am. Heading for Odessa. I came from El Paso. My mount died on me and I lost my way. Ran into an Injun yesterday who put me on the right trail. I tell ya, it ain't been easy."

Raider offered the man some dried beef.

The stranger readily accepted the food.

"Thanks. I got some whiskey if you want."

Raider started to accept the drink, but then he found that he wasn't in the mood after the first swallow.

"Don't like my liquor?" the stranger said good-naturedly.

Raider shook his head. "Tastes fine. I just don't have the urge." He looked up at the full moon, which was peeking between high clouds. "Somethin' 'bout this night," he said.

The stranger nodded. "I know what you mean. I heard all about it from those that I met on the trail."

Raider glanced at the traveler. "Heard 'bout what?"

The man eyed Raider. "You haven't heard?"

"No."

"About the Wolfbrand."

Raider chortled, wondering why he felt so uneasy. "No, pardner, that don't ring a bell. Less'n you mean an Injun that was killed a while back. I knew of a Sioux named Wolfbrand."

"This ain't no Injun. Not a live one, anyway."

Raider grimaced at the white-faced stranger. "What the devil are you talkin' 'bout?"

"The devil! Yeah, some say it's that. I'm hopin' this fire will keep it away."

Raider listened to the night, wondering if the stranger had lost his mind. Maybe some Indian had gotten hold of him, some Mescalero Apache with strange tales of monster men and snakes with wings. Raider had always been cautious of Mescaleros, even if they could be useful at times.

"They say it prowls these mountains," the stranger went on.

"Yeah?"

"The Wolfbrand," the man said. "It appears on the foreheads of men who are going to die—or in their hand."

Raider chortled. "You better lay off that bottle, pardner. And don't talk t' Injuns. They like t' rattle your head."

The man leaned forward, extending his hand. "Listen! The howling of the Wolfbrand."

Raider could only hear the wind. It would be best to keep moving, he thought.

"Listen," he said to the wide-eyed stranger. "If you're goin' to Odessa, maybe you oughta come along with me. I'm goin' there t' see a man named Chaney. Mebbe you know him. Jubal Chaney."

The man reached into his coat, which prompted Raider to go for his gun. But the man only came out with a wooden cross that he flashed at Raider. He told Raider to leave him alone.

"I see the sign of the Wolfbrand on your forehead," he muttered. "Keep away from me."

Raider figured he would be glad to get the hell away from the stranger. He led the gray away from the fire, never looking back.

When he had walked for a while, he stopped on the trail and

looked at the moon over his shoulder. Then he thought he heard it: the howling of a wolf.

Raider rushed back to the spot where the stranger had been sitting by his fire but the man was gone, disappeared. Burning in the fire was his wooden crucifix.

Raider drew his Colt and listened to the still air. Some of the sounds could have been interpreted as something escaping into the night. Of course, it was only the wind.

Maybe the stranger had decided to backtrack out of the mountains.

Raider figured it would be wise to make haste.

As Raider turned, he caught another glimpse of the cross in the flames. Why would the stranger run off without his good luck piece? Raider considered looking for him, but then he figured it was best to push on to Odessa. Maybe the stranger would turn up there.

The gray gelding snorted and pawed the ground. Raider held him still, listening, but there was no threat, at least not from the high slopes above.

Raider wheeled and led the animal away from the fire. He hoped to make it out of the mountains before the moon disappeared from the sky.

Odessa, Texas, was a pretty, whitewashed little town that didn't seem to be suffering too badly from the summer heat.

As Raider rode up the main avenue, several citizens marked his entrance into the settlement. He wondered how long it would take the local lawman to approach him. Raider would have to tell him about the disappearance of the eerie stranger in the mountains. For now, he would have to be content with getting the gray into a stable and finding a cool drink for himself.

He asked the livery man what day it was. After a short calculation, he decided that it had taken ten days to ride to Odessa. Not bad. The gray wasn't fast but it was steady.

The livery man directed him to the nearest saloon.

A few barflies noticed Raider's entrance. One of them left his perch at the bar. Raider knew that he was going for the sheriff.

Raider wasn't even halfway through his beer when the man with the badge pushed through the swinging doors.

He turned to smile at the lawman. "That didn't take long. Come on over here an' let me buy you a beer, sheriff."

The sheriff approached him cautiously. "I run a clean town, mister."

"Ain't lookin' t' dirty up nothin', sheriff. Name's Ray. I'm here on business with one o' your citizens."

The lawman eyed him through snake slits. "Your business partner got a name, Ray?"

"Chaney. Jubal Chaney."

The sheriff tensed.

One of the barflies laughed. "Chaney. That loco—"

The sheriff silenced him with a stern look. Then, to Raider: "I heard Chaney was going to bring in somebody to investigate his strange claims. Are you Wells Fargo?"

Raider shook his head. "Just a friend."

"That must make you a Pinkerton," the lawman rejoined.

"Hey, he's a Pinkerton!" came from one of the barflies.

Raider groaned. Now everyone would know a Pinkerton had come to town. There would be no chance to operate in secret.

"If you want my opinion," the sheriff went on, "Mr. Chaney brought it on himself. You might ask him if he got rid of them."

"Whoa, sheriff, slow down. I ain't had a chance t' speak t' Mr. Chaney yet. Mebbe you could—"

"The only thing I can tell you is, stay out of trouble while you're in my town. Chaney has a right to hire someone, but he doesn't have the right to break the law and neither do you. If I catch you up to something, I'll run you in as fast as anyone else."

The sheriff stormed out without giving his name. Raider didn't care. At least the constable wasn't going to get in his way. But he had stirred Raider's curiosity. The big man was now aching to meet Jubal Chaney.

He glanced toward the barflies. "Hey, I'll buy a drink for the first man who can tell me where t' find Jubal Chaney."

They were all ready to point him in the right direction.

Raider bought them a whole bottle.

They thanked him and told him to be careful around that loco Chaney.

Rather than ask what they meant, Raider decided to go see the man for himself.

CHAPTER SEVEN

Raider strode down a long, wooden sidewalk, passing houses that were adorned with petunias and bluebonnets. There were picket fences, blistered and flaking in the hot sun. When he cleared the houses, he looked to his right as he had been told by the barflies. The neighborhood seemed to turn darker as he gazed down the far side of town.

A long row of dark warehouses, battered by rain and sun, stretched toward a small grove of oaks and cottonwoods in the distance.

The sidewalk disappeared, so the big Pinkerton stuck to the side of the dirt street.

The barflies had told him that he would see Jubal Chaney's sign painted big and white on the side of his barn.

At first, Raider thought the seedy warehouses might be stables, but his nose told him that there were no animals about: no manure, no hay. He wondered what kind of business Jubal Chaney engaged in.

The man's name was emblazoned across a barn in white, cursive letters. Beneath the name was the bold word, MERCHANT, in heavy black capitals. The barn door was opened a crack so Raider slipped through sideways and waited for his eyes to focus in the shadows.

"Mr. Chaney?" he called. No one answered.

He stepped in a little farther. He saw boxes stacked high against the walls. Crates and kegs also formed neat rows. A loft was filled with merchandise. Chaney was a drummer.

"I'd stay real still if I was you, mister." The voice had come from behind him.

Raider glanced over his shoulder to see a man with a pistol in his hand. "Lookin' for Jubal Chaney," the big man said. "Would you be him?"

The man was big, round, with a thick slab encircling his gut. Hard eyes, reddish hair, sun-baked skin. Raider perceived the slightest trembling of the man's hand. He was nervous, as if he weren't used to drawing down on people.

"You sure you wasn't lookin' to steal from Mr. Chaney?" the man said.

Raider figured it was better just to blurt it out, what with the sheriff and half of Odessa already spreading the word. "I'm the Pinkerton agent hired by Mr. Chaney. Argue with that."

"How come I don't believe you?"

Raider chortled. "Well, you don't look too smart to me. Mebbe that's it. You ain't so bright."

"I could drop you right—unhh—"

The man hadn't even seen Raider's hand move. His eyes grew wide at the sight of Raider's Colt. Raider had drawn on him and could have killed him right there.

"Aw right," Raider challenged. "Let's see you drop me."

The man still didn't lower his weapon.

"Gonna make it rough for me," Raider went on, "explainin' how I had t' kill you, pardner. Now, drop me or drop that pistol."

The man snarled and tossed his revolver to the ground.

Raider waved the barrel of his gun. "Now, s'pose you tell me who the hell you are, stranger."

His face was aflame, beet-red, but he still managed to squawk out the angry words. "I work for Mr. Sharper."

"Who's he?"

"Owns these warehouses. I watch out for 'em."

"Whatta they call you?"

"Red."

Raider nodded. "That figgers, with that carrot top."

"I don't like that name!"

"Sorry." Raider holstered his weapon. "Hey, no hard feelin's."

"I cain't say the same."

The big man shrugged. "Then mebbe you better leave without your—"

Red lunged for his pistol. Raider jumped too, putting his foot on the pistol. It looked like an old Army Colt. The tall Pinkerton's hand was full of his revolver again.

"I thought I told you not t'—"

The rifle lever chortled above him. "Hold it right there."

Raider slowly lifted his hands toward the roof. He was pretty sure the voice had come from the loft behind his right shoulder. A quick turn might do it, if it had to be done.

The chubby Red scurried to his feet with the Army in hand. "Now I'm gonna—"

"You take it easy too, Red," the voice from the loft said. "This man is my guest."

Red scowled toward the loft. He wanted revenge now that the rifle was trained on Raider but the rifleman just motioned him out of the barn.

"You can turn around now, Pinkerton."

Raider eased in a circle, glancing at the shadows above him. He was startled at first by the strange pair of eyes that glared down at him. The face of Jubal Chaney had been framed by the shadows, but the eyes were alive with fire. As soon as the face emerged from the half-light, Raider saw the age and worry in the man's pale countenance.

Still, he nodded and tried to be polite. "Mr. Chaney, mind if I drop my hands?"

Chaney grunted and then looked at his rifle. "Sorry. I just have to be careful these days."

Raider dropped his gun into his holster. "I can see that."

"Wait there," Chaney said, disappearing into the stacks of merchandise.

He took a ladder at the back of the loft, a secret entrance and escape route out of his office, Raider would learn later.

Chaney reappeared and ushered Raider into a dark, cluttered office that was dominated by a large desk full of papers.

Chaney's strange, white-ringed eyes stared back at the big man from behind the desk. He was clad in black, had thin gray hair, and a manner that belied a lot of worry and disappointment. His hands were firm though, as he punctuated his deep, sonorous voice with gestures.

"Do you require whiskey?"

Raider shook his head. "Ain't been hankerin' for it much lately, but thanks just the same."

An enigmatic smile stretched across Chaney's thin lips. "Good. You're a gentleman. A man of few words."

"That's the way I like it," Raider replied. "S'pose you tell me a few about why you hired me."

Chaney sighed, leaning back, putting his hands together. "I'm a merchant, Mr. Raider."

"Just Raider."

"Very well. I'm a merchant. I buy merchandise and sell it for a higher price. Right now, in Odessa, a shortage of nails has allowed me to make a good profit on a wagon load I managed to bring in from El Paso."

"Business is good?"

Chaney frowned. "Fair and foul. My life profits in one minute and I lose all in the next."

Raider felt like prodding the man out of his dark mood, but he decided to hold back, at least until he found out why he had been summoned.

Chaney's wolf eyes stared straight at him. "You're wondering why you were hired."

The big man nodded. "Sort of."

"Murder most foul, Mr. Raider. My wife, my two sons: dead. And that stupid sheriff can't do anything but accuse me."

"He ain't locked you up yet," Raider offered.

"He has no proof that I'm guilty—or that I'm innocent. I can't really blame him, considering the circumstances surrounding the deaths."

Now they were getting somewhere. "What kinda circumstances?"

Chaney sighed and put his face in his hands. At first Raider thought he was going to cry. But then he looked up again.

"Raider, I still see them in my mind's eye. Their throats torn out, their bellies disembowled. Whatever killed them enjoyed it. All three of them. We thought the first death was a pack of wolves, but then—"

The big man sat up straight, as if he had heard something from the night before: a wolf howl; the missing stranger.

Chaney saw the change in his posture. "Are you all right, Raider?"

Raider remembered the cross burning in the fire. "Wolfbrand," he said aloud.

Chaney startled. "What did you say?"

"Wolfbrand."

Chaney gawked at him. "You've already heard—"

Raider told him about the man in the mountains.

Chaney shook his head. "If they find him at all, they'll find him dead, just like my family."

"What the hell is this Wolfbrand, anyway?"

Chaney put a hand to his forehead, like he was weary of something. "The sign of the wolf: a pentagram; five-pointed star."

"Is it Injun magic? Some kind of Mescalero medicine?"

Chaney shook his head. "No, it goes back to old legends from Europe. Werewolves, men who could transform themselves into wolves and run with a pack of natural animals. Supposedly, those who were bitten or scratched by a werewolf would change on the next full moon."

Raider tried to swallow but found that his mouth was dry. The moon had been full the night before. He had heard the cry. The wooden cross burned in the fire.

He shook his head. "Men changin' into wolves. Now there's somethin' I could never believe."

Chaney leaned forward. "Actually, lycanthropy has occurred in men. They don't really change into wolves, but they think they do."

"Sounds plum loco."

"Yes, it does."

Raider saw the sadness in the old man's eyes. "But you lost your family, so I don't reckon it seems that funny t' you."

"No, sir, it doesn't. I see them in my nightmares. Their throats are torn out. It could have been some kind of animal."

"And they were all murdered in the same way?" Raider asked.

Chaney nodded. "We tried to be careful after my youngest son was killed. But then—it didn't seem to matter."

"And they were killed here in town?"

Chaney shook his head. "No. I have a home out near Red Bluff, close to the Pecos River."

"Near the mountains."

"Yes, the mountains aren't too far away."

Raider's mind was starting to work. He needed a case like this. Something more challenging than a prisoner transfer or a routine manhunt. And Chaney was ready to give it up; a man at the rim of the canyon. Maybe the big man from Arkansas could find him some answers.

Raider made the old man tell it slowly, so he wouldn't leave anything out. His voice was cold, calm. He seemed almost dead. Something had spooked him—the Wolfbrand. Only it sounded pretty stupid to Raider. No man could change into a wolf, not even with enough peyote.

Chaney's youngest son was killed while hunting near the foothills. Two of their goats had been slain and dragged away, by coyotes, the boy thought. No one took heed when Bill Chaney mounted the pinto and headed off to hunt. The boy hunted all the time without incident.

Chaney's older son had been the one to find the body of his brother. The father came to view the corpse, but not in time to talk his oldest boy out of organizing a search for the wolf pack that had ripped out his brother's throat.

A week later, another search party found the second Chaney boy in the same condition. He had gotten lost in the mountains. The wolf pack apparently had killed him.

Chaney's wife, an elderly woman, was killed in her home, while the others were looking for her oldest son. Her throat bore the fang marks of a single animal, one creature, while the others had many bites all over them.

That had caused Raider to lean forward, frowning. "One animal? In the house?"

"That's when the rumors started," Chaney went on. "The Wolfbrand. A preacher over in Midland finally brought it back to me, when I was in Midland doing business. Though no one would speak of it in public, the local people of Midland feared the Wolfbrand would come their way."

Raider put his fingertips together, staring at nothing. "That boy in the hills said this mark o' the wolf appears whenever there's trouble. Did any o' your kin have the mark on 'em?"

"My wife," Chaney replied. "On her forehead."

"And that shit about the scratch makin' 'em into—what'd you call it?"

"A werewolf."

Raider laughed. "Where'd all this malarkey come from, anyway?"

Chaney shrugged. "It found its way around."

"Anybody seen this Wolfbrand?"

"There have been sightings," Chaney said. "The sheriff claimed that I did it myself, that I played the part so I wouldn't have to leave any of my money to my heirs."

"Well, don't be too hard on him, Jubal, he's just a lawman. He's bound t' come up with a stupid reason for all these goin's on. If he comes sniffin' 'round, just play like you wanna cooperate with him. It's better if he stays out of our way."

Chaney raised a thin eyebrow. "Does this mean you'll accept the case?"

Raider nodded. "I reckon. But you gotta know, Mr. Chaney, when I get to the bottom o' the barrel, I scrape off whatever's there. If you or anybody else is responsible, I gotta ring the bell on 'em."

Chaney sighed and threw out his hands. "If I were guilty, why would I hire you? Do you think my wealth means anything to me?"

Raider eyed him carefully. "I heard you didn't have the price of a telegram t' my boss."

"All right, business hasn't been good. And I haven't been good, either. It's all falling apart since my family died.'' He choked back the tears. ''But don't worry. When I sell all these kegs of nails, I'll be able to afford your agency's fee.''

The big man took it a step farther. ''Anybody 'round that might wanna see you go broke, Mr. Chaney?''

The old man gazed up with some hope, like Raider was the first person to take him seriously. ''Well, I am in direct competition with the man who owns this warehouse, John Sharper.''

''He a merchant like you?''

Chaney nodded. ''Yes, although we tried to avoid handling the same inventory. But since I've slowed down, he's been handling more and more of the items I carry. You know, pots, pans, coffeepots, forks, and knives.''

''Does he want you bad enough t' send the wolves after you?''

Chaney smiled a little. ''I don't think so. He's always been distant, but never hostile.''

''Sometimes you can find the most trouble in the still part o' the river,'' Raider offered. ''It's somethin' t' think about. Where'd that Red come from?''

''There was pilferage—''

Raider frowned. ''Come again.''

''Somebody was stealing from my warehouse, from all the warehouses. When I complained, Sharper brought in Red and there hasn't been any more thievery.''

''Mighta brought him in t' spy on you,'' Raider replied. ''Ever think o' that?''

Chaney wore a dubious expression. ''I don't think John Sharper would do that sort of thing.''

''Leave it t' me,'' Raider said. ''It's my case now. Two things: first, we gotta make sure you're safe. Have you been stayin' at your place by the Pecos?''

''No, I've been sleeping here, in town.''

The big man nodded. ''Good, that's prob'ly safest. You stay here while I have a look-see out at your ranch.''

''All right, if that's what you want.''

Raider asked for directions to Chaney's place.

''I'll have to sell it sooner or later,'' the old man said. ''I just can't bear the thought of living there.''

Raider stood up. "I better be gettin' started, Chaney. You stick close by. The sheriff has t' protect you if there's trouble."

"One moment, Raider."

The old boy took something from a desk drawer. "Here; cartridges. These are special bullets," Chaney offered. "I had them made myself. They're silver. Supposedly a silver bullet in the heart can kill a werewolf."

Raider patted his holster. "I'm just fine, Mr. Chaney. I don't b'lieve none o' that nonsense. Just keep 'em an' keep your rifle loaded. Somebody wanted your family dead an' they may be savin' you for last. Stayin' in town was a good notion."

"Why is that?"

"Whatever this thing is, it cain't operate 'round a lot o' people, otherwise it woulda come after you already. Now, mebbe it wanted your family, or mebbe you just got in the way. Fact is, it ain't bothered you since you come into town."

Chaney nodded appreciatively. "You're a brilliant man, Raider."

"No, sir, but I can tell my ass from a cactus, that's why I don't get stuck as much as other people."

"What are you going to do?"

Raider shrugged. "Poke around. Mebbe talk t' the sheriff. See if I can find somebody t' tell me 'bout the Wolfbrand."

"What kind of animal could it be?"

"A bear has a bite a lot like a wolf," Raider said. "Mebbe a grizzly wandered too far south. Or it could be a animal with rabies. I seen it afore. Mebbe even a dog. This man, Sharper, does he own any dogs?"

"Not that I know of. What are you getting at?"

Raider always got to the heart of the obvious. "Animals can be trained, Mr. Chaney. They'll do what you want 'em to if you treat 'em in the right way—or the wrong way."

"This is no domestic beast," Chaney warned. "You've never seen such evil destruction in your life."

"I wouldn't bet on it." He turned for the door.

"Be careful," Chaney told him.

Raider said he wouldn't have it any other way.

He promised to check back with the old man before the end of the day.

Raider shook his head as he came out of the warehouse, into the light of day. His initial urge was to head back to the Guadalupe Mountains to see if he could find the man who had told him about the Wolfbrand. Maybe that stranger was involved somehow.

He turned back toward town and started to walk along the line of warehouses. Best to start right in Odessa, since he was already there. He could go looking for shadows later, if he had to. Men made shadows and men concocted elaborate schemes to hurt each other. Raider had to find out who had conspired to kill Jubal Chaney's family.

Their throats torn out. Men who changed into wolves. He wondered if there were any Apaches around town. Sometimes they'd let them live off the reservation. A medicine man might be able to help.

Maybe it was a rabid animal. A horse or a burro might attack a man if they were sick enough. Maybe it was a mad dog with a foaming mouth.

No! The damned thing had come into Chaney's house to kill his wife. It had enough smarts to stalk its prey. It— Raider realized that he was thinking of it as a monster. He had seen monsters before and they were always man-made.

Best to get into town and talk to the sheriff again. Then he could—

Something fell behind him. The thud was quick and loud.

Raider spun with his Colt, drawing down on a sack of flour that had landed behind him. The sack had split and white dust was flying around him. Laughter came from a loft above.

He looked up at the man named Red.

"Sorry, Pinkerton, it just slipped out of my hand."

He was holding a pitchfork.

Raider fired and sawed the pitchfork's handle into two pieces.

Red jumped back, shaking his hand. "That stung."

"You're lucky I didn't kill you!" Raider snarled. "I oughta pull you down from there an' whip your ass."

Red pointed a finger at him. "You ain't man enough!"

"Name the time and place, gopher face."

Before the red-haired man could answer the challenge, the door opened and a man came out of the warehouse with a shotgun in hand. "What seems to be the trouble?" he asked.

Raider saw that he was well dressed; smooth and dapper. His face was calm but the scattergun seemed serious enough. Raider still held the Colt in hand, which made for respect on all sides.

"Your man here has a truck with me," Raider said. "He's tryin' t' pick a fight. Threw that flour sack at me."

"Slipped out of my hand—"

The dapper man glanced up at Red. "Shut up." Then, to Raider: "Perhaps I should introduce myself. I'm John Sharper."

Raider holstered the Colt and extended his hand. "Call me Raider. I'm helpin' out Mr. Chaney for the time bein'."

Sharper's smile was cool. "The Pinkerton."

Raider glared straight at him. "Chaney's come on hard times, Sharper. Seems that'd help you."

Sharper gave a faint laugh, averting his dark eyes. "I've always held the balance between myself and Chaney. Now that he's having trouble, I have no choice but to provide the town of Odessa with certain necessities."

"Well," Raider rejoined, "I'm providin' somethin' too, Sharper. I sure hope you don't get in the way."

"On the contrary." The voice was slick as a snail's belly. "If I can be of any help to you, feel free to ask. Always glad to help a colleague in trouble. It's the professional way."

They stared at each other until Sharper drew away.

From the loft, Red cried: "Hey, you ain't gonna let him—"

Sharper fixed a stern eye on the man. "I've heard enough from you today. Get about your business."

Red whined but limped away from the loft door.

Sharper peered at Raider again. "If he gives you any more trouble, feel free to tell me. I'll fire him at once."

"Join me for a drink at the saloon?" Raider asked.

The merchant shook his head. "No. I have work to do. Good day."

He went back into the warehouse.

Raider exhaled and tipped back his Stetson. Odessa was turning out to be a pretty creepy town. There was too much to ponder in a couple of hours. He'd have to think about it for a while before he made a move.

CHAPTER EIGHT

Raider needed a beer. The wind had picked up, making the air gritty with blowing dust. He wasn't in the mood for hard liquor, but a draft might surely take the edge off.

When he pushed through the swinging doors of the saloon, the sheriff turned back from the bar and looked at him.

Raider tipped his hat and said, "Just the man I wanted t' see."

The sheriff grimaced. "Me?"

Raider strode toward the bar, sliding next to the lawman. "Whatta they call you, pardner?"

"Daniels," the sheriff replied. "Bit Daniels."

Raider gestured to the lawman's empty glass. "Let me buy you one."

Daniels eyed him suspiciously. "I'm drinkin' sarsaparilla."

"Then give him one, barkeep, an' draw me a long one."

"Sarsaparilla?" the bartender asked.

"No," Raider replied, "real beer."

"Got a natural spring in the basement," the bartender said enthusiastically, "keeps the beer cold."

"I'll take your word for it."

Sheriff Daniels wasn't sure what to think. "When did we become buddies, Pinkerton?"

"We're both on the same side now," Raider offered. "I'm gonna have a look after the Chaney killin's."

Daniels sighed. "I saw it comin'."

"I need t' know what you think, sheriff. And not that stuff about Chaney gettin' rid of his heirs."

The bartender put their drinks in front of them. Raider dropped a dollar on the counter. The barkeep started to say something, but a stern look from the black-eyed Pinkerton turned him away.

He regarded Daniels, a weary-looking lawman. "I'm listenin', Bit."

After a moment, the sheriff replied, "I ain't sure what the hell happened, big man. Three people were killed and there don't seem to be any reason."

"Had any Injun trouble out that way?"

"Not since I been sheriff."

Raider lifted the mug, taking a long pull. "Anybody have a truck against the Chaneys?"

"Not that I know of."

"How 'bout John Sharper?"

Daniels squinted at him. "You get around pretty good."

Raider shrugged. "I try. Seems Sharper is gettin' the benefits from Chaney's troubles."

"I thought of that," Daniels replied soberly. "But Sharper ain't involved. I can't find a thing against him."

Raider drained the mug and plopped it on the counter. "Mebbe I can."

The sheriff pointed a finger at him. "Don't go stirrin' up my town."

"It needs t' be stirred, leastways till somethin' floats t' the top. An' it always does, Bit, as long as I'm the one who's stirrin'."

Daniels found a strange kind of logic in Raider's delivery. He rested his hands against the bar and asked for a whiskey. There was a real problem and Bit was worried that it might come into

Odessa. He told Raider, between sips of the red-eye, about the bodies of the Chaney family.

"Could've been a rabid animal," Raider offered.

"Hmm. Didn't think of that."

"The woman, Mrs. Chaney: He says she was killed by a single animal. One creature. Did you look for tracks at the Chaney place?"

The lawman shook his head. "By the time I got there, the place was pretty well trampled."

Raider saved the best for last. "What about all this Wolfbrand stuff? Men changin' into animals an' such."

"You wouldn't be so calm if you had seen those bodies."

"I wish I could see 'em," the big man rejoined. "But I ain't one for diggin' up graves."

A shudder from the lawman. "Me neither."

Raider asked for another beer. Then, to the lawman: "Okay, Daniels, what's it gonna be?"

"I don't understand."

"You gonna fight me?" Raider asked. "Or are you gonna let me find out what really happened to the Chaneys?"

The lawman tensed to give his answer, but he never got it out.

A loud clamor resonated from the street, calling the attention of both men to the entrance. From the noise involved, Raider figured it to be at least a fistfight. But it was only one old lady who burst through the swinging doors.

Daniels rolled his eyes and grimaced. "The widow Henshaw. You want to handle her, Pinkerton?"

"No, I seen them kind afore. I'll shoot her for you, if you promise you won't hang me."

The elderly woman whirled through the barroom like a cyclone. She was ranting and raving. She finally began to pound the sheriff with a sewing bag.

"Just tell me what it is, Widow Henshaw!"

Raider had retreated to the other end of the bar, taking his beer with him. He was afraid of old widow ladies. There wasn't much a man could do to stop them once they got going.

"I have never in my life, Sheriff Daniels, had to put up with this kind of insult to a widow woman, living alone as I do—"

Daniels was stunned and obviously in the mood for a second

drink. Raider hated to see lawmen become tipplers, but he had some sympathy for them. Being a sheriff could drive a man to drink.

"What is it, Widow Henshaw?"

She shook her bag at him. "It's that John Sharper!"

Raider leaned forward a little, listening to her.

"He's keeping me awake all night. I haven't had a good night's sleep in a week!"

"What's he doing to keep you awake?"

She wasn't going to make it easy on the sheriff, or anyone else for that matter. "His house is right behind mine, sheriff. I didn't object when he moved in, because he's such a nice young man."

"Well, he is that," Daniels offered, sinking deeper toward a shot of red-eye. "But he's keepin' you awake now?"

"It's those dogs!"

Raider's eyes widened.

"They bark night and day."

Daniels frowned. "Dogs? I didn't know Sharper had any dogs."

Raider felt his body begin to tingle. It was almost like being near a pretty woman. He hadn't been in town a whole day and things were already working out—at least on the surface. Best to take it slowly, the way he did with Consuela.

"He must have a pack of them over there," the Widow Henshaw went on. "Bark, bark, bark. Why if my husband Hiram—who was one of the founders of this town—was alive, he'd be furious."

"I'm sure he was—"

"So you had better have a talk with John Sharper, or I'll see to it that the town council hears about this!"

She turned and blew out the same way she had come in.

Raider eased back down the bar. "Let me buy you a snort, Daniels. Looks like she took all of the wind outta you."

The sheriff didn't decline the big man's generosity. He seemed to steady when the hooch went down. His hands were still trembling a little.

"I used to be a marshal," Daniels said sadly, "up in New Mexico. I thought this would be better, sheriffin' I mean, but I kind of miss the old days. No widows back then."

Raider shook his head, exhaling. "You don't see it, do you, Bit? It's right under your nose, but you don't see it."

"See what?"

"Dogs!" Raider cried. "A pack of 'em. And Sharper's got 'em at his place. Sharper, the man who's pickin' up the slack for Chaney."

The lawman put a hand to his forehead. "My God. You're right. Hell, what am I gonna do?"

Raider leaned a little closer to him. "Turn me loose, sheriff. Let me figger it out. All you have t' do is look the other way. Swallow your pride. Hell, I'll even let you take all the credit at the end, so the town council will get off your back."

"You ain't gonna break the law, are you?"

The big man grinned. "Not so's you'd notice, sheriff."

"Do it. But hear this. If you break the law, I'll have to lock you up."

Raider said that all he wanted to do was catch the thing that had killed Jubal Chaney's kin.

Jubal Chaney's warehouse was dark when Raider returned to check in with the old man.

He eased through the shadows, slowly opening the office door. His hand hovered over the butt of his Colt. The gray-haired merchant sat slumped behind his desk.

For a moment, Raider thought he was dead. Chaney's skin had turned pale and he wasn't stirring. Then he made a chortling noise, sitting up with eyes open, gawking at Raider.

"Who is it?"

"The Pinkerton."

Chaney chortled and coughed as he torched an oil lamp. "I fell off to sleep," he said.

"If I wanted t' plug you, Chaney, I coulda done it in a hurry."

"You would be doing me a favor. Any luck?"

Raider sat down, stretching his long legs in front of him. "Well, the sheriff don't really think you did it—kill your kin, I mean. He ain't sure what happened, just like the rest of us."

Chaney seemed unmoved by this news. "Anything else?"

"I'm free to have a look 'round, and so far I been steppin' in shit all the way—good luck, I mean. I found out today that John Sharper has some dogs at his place."

"Dogs?"

Raider nodded. "Animals. Some widow lady was complainin' that the barkin' had kept her awake."

Chaney sat up straighter. "That'd be Ruth Henshaw. Her place is next to Sharper's house. The two places are considered the best properties in town."

"Well," the big man replied, "all you have t' do is tell me how t' get there—"

The moon rose full and bright over the horizon. Raider stepped out of Jubal Chaney's warehouse, into a cool night. A breeze was blowing down from the north. A slight haze was in the air. Maybe it would rain the next day.

He started down the street, toward the grove of oaks and cottonwoods that lay another five hundred yards to the east.

Chaney had told him that the widow was on one side of the property and Sharper was on the other. The forest lay between their houses. Neither dwelling was visible from the road, as they both were hidden by the trees.

Raider hesitated at the edge of the grove. If he ran across the widow's place, she might see him and go running to the sheriff. He didn't want that. On the other hand, if Sharper saw him, he might sick a pack of dogs on him.

Still, he had to see for himself and this was the best way. Sharper's place lay to the left. There wasn't a marked path, but the trees weren't too thick. But something kept him at the edge of the road.

The wind picked up, stirring the leaves.

Raider peered between the tree trunks, looking for light from the Sharper place. Chaney had described it as a low-walled stucco hacienda, a lot like the places Raider had seen in Mexico.

He knew he had to make his way through the grove so he started in, calculating each step.

He saw the lights from the house glowing ahead of him. Then he heard the howling. Some animal shrieked in agony, like a banshee or a demon from Hell.

Raider drew his Colt and kept going, wondering what the hell he was going to find at the other end of the woods.

He kept low in the trees, moving through the shadows like an animal himself. Raider remembered when he had been hunting as a boy, in the hills of Arkansas. He'd hear a single leaf shiver, see the last twitch of a fox tail, and then watch as the fox hid behind a bush that wasn't any thicker than a rat's tail. It was eerie how animals could hide so much better than men. He hunkered low in the bushes. He could see the hacienda now. The howling had stopped, but the wind still stirred in the trees above him.

For a while he studied the front of the house, thinking that he would have to get a higher vantage point if he intended to look down into the courtyard of the place. Seeing in posed no problem, especially with the full moon, but he'd have to be able to peer over the wall.

Easing out of the woods, he started crawling toward a thick oak tree that rose at the edge of the grove. It would be easy to climb. Maybe he could get a peek from there.

When he reached the base of the oak tree, he slid around into the shadows. He stood up, but he never got a chance to look for a hold to climb. The animal was coming straight for him. He heard it first, then caught the glimmer of a blur as the canine shape lunged through the air. He reached for his Colt, but he knew there wasn't enough time to get it out of the holster.

The dog-shape was a rapidly charging shadow, its teeth bared at the big man. He saw its drooling maw and flashing eyes that seemed to glow.

His only aim was to draw the Colt, to get off one shot, but finally it didn't matter.

Another shot erupted in the night. From the corner of his eye, Raider saw the flash of a rifle muzzle. The dark form of the dog buckled and fell to the ground, twitching and yelping.

Raider finished it with a slug to the head. Then he turned in the direction of the rifle muzzle.

John Sharper came toward him with the rifle pointed straight at him. "What the devil are you doing on my land?"

"I got lost," Raider lied. "Figgered to ask you for directions. You said you'd help me if I needed it."

Sharper nodded absently, looking down at the dead animal. "Sorry, but he got out."

Raider bent to look at the canine corpse.

"No," Sharper said. "Don't touch him. I think he may have rabies. I hate to think it, but he might."

Raider eased back. "Damn."

He didn't want to say anything right away. It might look too obvious. He just wanted to get the hell back to town before Sharper suspected anything.

"I have two just like him," Sharper said. "Bloodhounds. I had hoped they'd be able to live in this damnable Texas climate, but I think it's proved too much for them."

Raider holstered his Colt. "Well, thanks for shootin' him."

"You finished him off," Sharper replied. "He might have gotten away. That would have been trouble. I've had enough of that already. The widow on the other side of the grove said she heard them barking last night. She complained to the sheriff."

Raider eyed him, feeling like the whole thing was wrong somehow.

"I'm going to have to shoot the other two now," Sharper said, a puzzling smile on his thin lips. "Can't take a chance."

"Where you think they picked up the bad bite?" Raider asked.

Sharper pointed west. "I have a cabin in the mountains. I kept the dogs there all summer, because it's cooler. I think one of them was bitten by a raccoon or a badger but I can't be sure."

"So you're gonna shoot the other two?"

Sharper glanced sideways at him. "Yes, why would I want to have them live? They'd only pose a threat to every animal in this part of the state. It's the civic thing to do."

Raider was steaming inside. He wanted to stop this man from destroying the evidence. That was the real reason Sharper had chosen to kill the animals. With the dogs dead, there would be no proof.

"Your place up near Red Bluff?" he asked the merchant.

Sharper nodded. "Not far. Why?"

Raider started to turn. "Reckon I better get back t' town."

He wanted to bring the sheriff before the dogs were destroyed or at least bring Daniels to see the dead ones. It was best to hurry.

"Where are you going?" Sharper asked.

Raider turned to pay respects to the rifle, even if the bore was aimed at the ground. "Back t' town."

Sharper lifted the Winchester, but only to point. "Take the road. It'll be easier."

The big Pinkerton hurried away.

He was almost to the main road when he heard the two shots. He glanced over his shoulder to see the flame-glow as the fire rose in the courtyard of the hacienda. The Widow Henshaw would no longer have any reason to complain. John Sharper seemed to be burning the evidence.

CHAPTER NINE

Raider burst into the sheriff's office, startling Bit Daniels.

The lawman gaped at the big Pinkerton who tried to catch his breath. Raider had run all the way from Sharper's place. He knew they had to move quickly, before the evidence was gone.

"Dogs," he told Daniels, "three of 'em. Sharper says they all have rabies, so he's tryin' t' kill 'em in a hurry."

Daniels rubbed his chin. "Rabies, huh?"

"One of those hounds tried to attack me."

The sheriff gave him the once-over. "Didn't seem to do too much damage. You ain't bleedin' nowhere."

Raider waved him off. "Sheriff, you gotta go with me now. See what he's doin'. If you don't hurry, we'll never pin him down."

Daniels reluctantly rose from behind his desk. "This had better be good, Pinkerton. Sharper's never caused any trouble before."

"Just get a move on," the big man replied, "afore it's too late."

Both of them rode silently toward Sharper's place in Daniel's buggy. When they turned onto the narrow road that led to the hacienda, Raider saw that the fire was still burning. He knew then that nothing would come of it, but he had to press on, to show the merchant that he was on to him.

As they approached the front entrance of the hacienda, a man met them at the door. He was dark-skinned, Mexican probably. He seemed to be expecting them.

Instead of leading Raider and the sheriff through the house, the man ushered them around the side of the building, delivering them into the back courtyard. John Sharper stood at the edge of a big bonfire, still holding his rifle. He had a sad, weary expression on his face.

The sheriff nodded and tipped his hat. "Evenin', Mr. Sharper. Sorry to bother you but—"

Sharper turned to look at Raider. "I understand. Our tall friend here no doubt regaled you with tales of rabid hounds."

Daniels blushed and looked away. "Yeah, well—"

Raider kept his eyes on Sharper. "Rabies ain't what I was worried 'bout."

"Raider!" the sheriff barked.

"I might as well say it," the big man went on. "Chaney's kin was killed by animals. Hounds mebbe. Hounds like you're burnin' in that fire."

Sharper shrugged. "I see what you're getting at, but it isn't true. These dogs were for hunting. Deer hunting."

Raider wasn't ready to give up. "Mebbe, but if that's so, why're you so headstrong 'bout killin' 'em?"

"I told you," the merchant said coldly. "Rabies. Besides, if I had wanted to cover up something, why would I have saved you from that rabid hound that almost attacked you, Pinkerton?"

"To make it look good for yourself," Raider replied. "Make it look like you had nothin' t' hide. T' throw me off the trail."

Sheriff Daniels was watching Sharper closely. "He does make some sense, Mr. Sharper. You did have these dogs and you are makin' good on Chaney's trouble. Care to answer for yourself?"

Sharper stiffened. "I don't have to answer anything. The facts speak for themselves."

Raider started to interject something, but the merchant cut him off.

"However, if you two gentlemen would like to join me in a libation, a drink of whiskey if you will, then I shall be happy to answer any questions you have about my activities of late."

Daniels turned to Raider. "I say we listen to him," the sheriff offered.

The big man nodded, keeping his eye on the rifle. Sharper was quick. He hadn't left them much choice but to listen to him. Raider just hoped he could catch him in a lie.

Sheriff Daniels sipped the fine whiskey that had been poured by their host. Raider also took a shot, but he didn't drink. He didn't trust the dapper gentleman. So far everything pointed to misdeeds by the merchant.

They had taken chairs in a dimly lighted parlor. It wasn't as fancy as Raider had figured it would be. The Mexican man served the bottle of whiskey and then left them alone.

Sharper stood next to a dark fireplace. "It's seldom cool enough for a fire down this way," he said calmly. "Sometimes I wonder why I ever left St. Louis." He looked at Raider. "That's right, Mr. Pinkerton, St. Louis. If you want to check on me, you can contact a Mr. Wilson of the Overland Mercantile Company. I worked for him for five years before I headed south."

"An' just why did you come t' Texas?" Raider asked.

The sheriff gawked at him. "That ain't none of your business—"

Sharper smiled. "It's quite all right, sheriff. To answer your question, I came to Texas because I thought there would be some opportunities here that no longer existed in Missouri. I wanted my own company, to find a place that needed a merchant."

"Only Odessa already had one—name of Chaney."

"Fair enough," Sharper went on. "But as I told you before, Chaney and I had an agreement. With the business over in Midland and the business right here in Odessa, there was plenty to go around. We agreed, as I said, to carry different stock. Up until the tragedy of the Chaney family—"

"A tragedy that was caused by animals," Raider challenged. "Wolves, or dogs. Mebbe bloodhounds."

He expected to get a rise out of the merchant, but Sharper only shook his head.

The sheriff seemed more interested now. "He does have a point, Mr. Sharper. You did have those dogs. And you have more business now that Chaney has fallen on hard times."

"That hound was coming straight for me," Raider contended. "Like it was used t' attackin' people."

Sharper never missed a beat. "Like I said, the animal was rabid. I had to destroy it, along with the others."

Daniels seemed to be thinking now. "Ya know, Mr. Sharper, seems I never knew you to be much of a hunter. Why'd you really have them dogs?"

Raider smiled. "Answer the sheriff, John."

Sharper sighed and put down his whiskey glass. "All right, you caught me in a white lie. I've never been hunting in my life. I bought those dogs to protect me from the same monster that killed Chaney's family. When I heard about the first death, I became scared. I'm not used to such things. We don't have wolf packs in St. Louis."

Raider sat up sharply. "How'd you know it was a wolf pack?"

"What else could it be?" Sharper replied. "I heard about the way their throats were ripped out. Only a wolf could do that."

Raider leaned back in the chair. "Not necessarily. It coulda been a mountain lion or a bear."

"Or a bloodhound," the sheriff chimed in.

Sharper laughed a little. "I suppose it doesn't look too good for me. But I was nowhere near the Chaney place when any of the murders occurred. I can prove that. Just asked my hired man. Rodrigo can vouch for me."

He started to call the man in to testify.

Raider stopped him. "Don't fret, Sharper. We ain't gonna arrest you. Are we, sheriff?"

Daniels looked puzzled. "Well, I don't know—"

"Besides," Raider went on, smiling at the merchant, "if Mr. Sharper here wanted t' kill somebody, it woulda been Chaney hisself. Ain't that right, John?"

Sharper also seemed baffled. "I suppose. Just what are you getting at, Pinkerton?"

Raider stood up. "Just this, Sharper. Me and the sheriff'll be goin' now. An' we won't be back t' bother ya."

"Then you believe me?"

Raider started toward the door. "Come on, Bit. We don't wanna bedevil this fine citizen anymore. He's told us all we need t' know."

Daniels put down his drink and followed the big man.

Sharper watched them go, a dubious expression on his face.

Raider shut the door behind him.

"Why'd you up and leave like that?" the sheriff asked.

Raider climbed into the seat of the buggy. "Just get this wreck to the edge o' the road an' find a place t' stop."

The sheriff turned the buggy around and headed for the main road.

"Doggone it, Pinkerton, you had him in that lie about the dogs. Why'd you let him off the hook?"

Raider exhaled. "We cain't just take him in, Bit. Even if the evidence does point to him, he can say his piece in court and the jury might b'lieve him. No, he ain't hung hisself—yet. Just keep movin'."

When they had cleared Sharper's property, the sheriff guided the buggy into a stand of bushes where the wagon could not be seen.

Raider kept his eyes trained in the direction of the hacienda.

"What're you lookin' for?" the sheriff asked.

"I ain't sure. A rider mebbe."

In the light of the moon, they watched for the better part of an hour. No one rode away from the hacienda. Not from the front entrance, anyway.

The sheriff was getting antsy. "I thought you were gonna keep me out of this, Pinkerton."

Raider shrugged. "I did say that, Bit. But think 'bout how long it'll take the good citizens of Odessa t' elect a new sheriff when the first body turns up. So far you've been able t' protect 'em from the wolf-monster. But a few bodies with no throats'll get 'em riled up."

Daniels swallowed, his throat suddenly dry. "Aw right. I reckon I see what you mean."

Raider jumped off the buggy. "Stay here another hour. If nothin' happens, meet me back at Chaney's warehouse. I gotta see if he's okay."

The sheriff started to protest.

Raider drew a finger across his throat. "Don't take long t' nail together a ballot box, Daniels."

The sheriff said he'd wait another hour.

With the full moon over his shoulder, Raider could see his own shadow moving along the ground.

It was a windy night, the kind that made hearing almost impossible. Were those footsteps following him back to town? Dull, half-heard clomps that made him turn around and look behind him, but no one was there.

So he hurried along, wondering if Sharper had another set of dogs stashed somewhere. Of course, if the merchant was really the culprit—and Raider thought for sure he was—then he'd lay low for a while, keep his business private. Maybe there was some way to smoke him out.

He thought he heard the footsteps again. Raider turned, but there was nothing in the shadows. Sweat dripped off his face. This damned thing had him spooked.

He remembered the flashing eyes of the bloodhound. He wondered if the victims had witnessed the same thing. Jubal Chaney's kin had died at the hands of some ferocious animal. Maybe they hadn't even seen it coming.

When he reached Chaney's warehouse, he eased into the darkness, listening for signs of the old man. The place was quiet. No light or movement.

"Chaney?"

Was the old boy asleep in his office? Raider stepped carefully toward the office door.

The air was hot, clammy.

Something bumped to his right. He turned, drawing his Colt.

But then something struck him in the head and he went down on the floor of the warehouse.

The glancing blow felled him, but it did not knock him out.

Raider rolled to his left, escaping the boot-toe that kicked at his ribs. A man was after him, not a monster. Unless monsters wore boots.

He jumped up with the Colt in hand.

The man kept coming.

Raider swung his pistol, catching the assailant on the side of the head. The man went down at his feet. Raider dipped a shoulder and put the bore of his pistol against the intruder's temple.

"You ain't gonna move again, are you?"

The man on the ground grunted.

Raider's eyes lifted when he heard the scratching sound. A match glowed to life. Across the warehouse, Jubal Chaney stuck the flame to the wick of an oil lamp. "What the devil is going on here?"

Raider called him over. "Somebody tried t' bushwhack me, an' I got a good idea who it is."

When Chaney came closer with the lamp, they both saw the figure on the ground. It was the man named Red. He lay spread-eagled, with his face in the dirt.

"Red!" Chaney cried. "What are you doing in here?"

"I seen him come in," the man muttered. "I thought he was stealin'. Ain't that what Mr. Sharper hired me for?"

Raider kept the barrel of the gun on Red's temple. "What else did he hire you for? To spy on Mr. Chaney here?"

"No, he ain't done it!"

"Whatta you know 'bout them dogs?" the big man pressed. "Come on, tell me. I know you're in on it."

"Don't know nothin' about it," Red insisted. "I was hired to watch the warehouse. That's all."

Chaney waved the lamp in a trembling hand. "Let him up."

Raider jerked the pudgy man to his feet. "You're a brave one, Red. Pretty good at bushwhackin' people in the dark."

"I'd take you in a fair fight the best day you ever lived!"

Raider holstered the Colt. "I'm ready."

Red hesitated. "You mean now?"

"Why not?" the big man challenged. "Chaney here can watch, make sure it's fair."

Chaney shook his head. "Raider, I don't think—"

"Aw, don't worry, Chaney. Red here is a chicken. He don't wanna toe up, not fair an' square."

"I'll fight you anytime!"

Chaney still had doubts.

Raider took him aside, making sure that he kept an eye on Red. "Look here, Jubal, if I whup him pretty good, he might talk. Tell us what he really knows. Sometimes a man'll open his mouth after he's had a whuppin'."

Chaney reluctantly agreed.

Raider turned back to the stocky man, who was glaring at him. "So, what'll it be, Red? You wanna toe it up, or you wanna slide outta here like the sidewinder you really are?"

Red scowled and told the big man from Arkansas that he was ready to fight.

Chaney stood with the lamp in his hand. He was white-faced. He didn't need any more trouble, but here it was, in the form of a six-foot Pinkerton who drew a line in the dirt with his toe.

"The loser is the first man who cain't toe the mark," Raider told the red-haired man.

Red pointed at the hogleg on Raider's hip. "You gonna wear your gun?"

Raider unbuckled the belt and handed it to Chaney. "If he cheats, shoot him."

Chaney sighed. "Just get it over with."

"Toe up, Red."

"You first, Pinkerton."

Raider was about to put his foot on the mark when Red rushed straight for him. He was too close for Raider to dodge him. The tackle sent Raider to the dirt with a thud.

Red grabbed his ear and tried to bite him.

Figuring the fight was not going to be fair, Raider used a thumb to gouge Red in the eye.

The fat man rolled off him, hollering at the top of his lungs. "That ain't right!"

Raider had regained his balance. "Come on, pork barrel. See if you can toe up without cheatin'."

Red staggered to his feet, holding a hand to his eye. "I cain't see. You poked me in the eye."

"Shoulda thought 'bout that 'fore you tried t' chaw off my ear."

Red staggered toward the big man, holding his eye. Raider saw it coming this time. When the fat man was close enough, he came out of his posture and swung a hard right hand at Raider.

Raider drew back in time to avoid the blow.

The force of the punch threw Red off balance, making his gut an easy target for an uppercut by the tall Pinkerton.

Ribs cracked. Red made a grunting sound and sank to one knee. Raider didn't let him up. He kicked hard with his boot, catching Red in the chest. Red fell on his back, groaning.

"Had enough?"

The man only made a defeated sound.

Chaney held the lamp over him. "Is he dead?"

"No," Raider replied. "He ain't dead."

He grabbed the front of Red's shirt. "Talk, you tub o' guts. Why'd Sharper really hire you?"

Blood trickled down the man's chin.

Raider shook him again. "Come on, Red. You know Sharper hired you t' spy on Chaney. Tell the truth."

"Okay, okay. Just let me go."

As soon as Raider released his grip, Red came up with a handful of dust. He threw the dirt straight into the big man's face. Raider lost his vision for a moment and the fat man was on him.

Red drove a fist into Raider's face. The stunning blow caught him between the eyes. He fell backward, feeling his head spin.

Red jumped on him and they rolled across the floor, grappling in the dirt. This time it was Raider who sank his teeth into the man's earlobe. Red screamed and grabbed the side of his head. Raider managed to get away from him and regain his feet.

Red lay on the floor of the warehouse, whining. "You bit me!"

Raider moved toward him. "An' I ain't finished."

"Please," the fat man whimpered, "no more."

"You ready t' talk?" Raider asked.

Chaney moved next to him. "I want this to stop."

Red tried to stand again. "I ain't talkin'."

He backed toward the crates and boxes that were stacked against the wall. Blood trickled between his fingers. Raider had almost bitten off his ear. Red didn't like the taste of his own medicine.

"Talk or fight," the big man challenged.

Red rushed him again.

Chaney stepped back, making a gasping noise.

Raider sidestepped him and managed to give him kick in the backside.

Red slammed against the crates on the other wall. He turned quickly with his fist clenched. Hatred burned in his piggish eyes.

"You're gonna get it now, Pinkerton. I'm gonna tear you apart."

Raider lifted his own hands. "Let's see what you got, fat boy."

They began to circle.

Red lunged first, striking a harmless blow that caught Raider on the shoulder. The fat man was off balance. His face was right there.

The big man countered with a hard left to the side of the man's head.

Red felt the blow. He staggered back again, but then he started coming. His fists swung wildly in the air, missing with every strike.

Raider peppered his face with rights and lefts, but the fat man still did not go down. He was tough. The tall Pinkerton had to give him that.

"Enough," Chaney said. "He's beaten."

"Ain't done it!" Red cried.

Raider stood his ground. "I'm right here, fat boy."

Red lunged with an awkward blow.

Raider brought up a roundhouse haymaker, catching the man's chin with the full force of the punch.

His fist turned Red in circles.

The fat man staggered again toward the crates on the wall.

Raider and Chaney both expected him to go down.

But instead, he only rested for a moment on one knee.

When Red came back up, he had a pry bar in his hand. It was short and heavy, the kind of tool used to open crates. He waved it at Raider.

"You're gonna get yours now, Pinkerton."

Chaney held out the holster to Raider. "Here, take your gun."

Raider shook his head. "No, this gob o' spit is mine. Let him use that iron if he needs it."

"I'm gonna kill you!"

He stalked Raider, swinging the pry bar.

But every time Red swung, the iron missed Raider's head. He was too quick for the red-haired bushwhacker. And it made Red madder and madder.

"You son of a bitch!"

He swung again, but Raider was faster. He hit Red in the gut, causing him to bend over. Raider moved back, watching him.

"Give it up, Red. You ain't got it in you."

But the fat man made a last, desperate move.

Raider lashed out, kicking him in the chest.

Then it happened.

Raider felt his toe catch in the front of the man's shirt.

His foot was trapped for a moment, allowing Red to get a grip on his ankle.

Raider lost his balance and went down again, this time with the fat man standing over him.

Red lifted the pry bar to strike him.

Raider tried to roll away, but the man still held his foot.

He lifted his hand to try to stop the blow.

Red's hand fell with the bar, aiming straight for the big man's head.

"The pistol!" Raider cried to Chaney.

Red smiled, like it was over.

Then a pistol erupted, only it wasn't Chaney who had shot.

Red grabbed his wrist and dropped the pry bar.

Blood gushed from the back of his hand.

Raider glanced over to see Bit Daniels with a smoking revolver in his hand. He jumped to his feet and nodded to the sheriff. Daniels came into the shadows of the warehouse.

"What the hell is goin' on here?" he asked.

Raider nodded to his wounded attacker. "Just a little beef twixt me an' Red here. I had him till I caught my foot in his shirt."

"Looks like he was cheatin' to me," Daniels said.

Chaney nodded as he handed Raider his holster. "He was cheating. But it's over now. Thank God."

Raider looked at the fat man, who bled into the dust. "You wanna tell us why Sharper really hired you?"

Red didn't have much to say.

"I oughta lock him up," Daniels said.

Raider glanced at the sheriff. "Hey, what're you doin' here anyway, Daniels? You're s'posed t' be watchin' the hacienda."

"I was," the sheriff replied, his weapon still pointed at Red. "Till they left there."

Raider's eyes opened wide. "They?"

"Sharper and the Mexican," Daniels replied. "They both took off to the west about ten minutes ago. I think I know where they're going, too."

"Good; you can tell me an' then you can lock up ol' Red here."

"Lock me up?" the bleeding man whined.

"I'm goin' with you," the sheriff replied.

"No. Stay here with Chaney. Make sure he's safe."

"But—"

Raider told him he could handle it alone. First he had to get his horse from the livery. Then he would be on his way, following Sharper and his manservant. They were going to destroy more evidence, he figured.

"I still can't believe Sharper would do this to me," Chaney offered.

Raider said he would find out for sure tonight. It wouldn't be hard to follow them, not with the full moon to light his way.

CHAPTER TEN

They hurried toward the sheriff's office, to look at his maps. Mr. Chaney had volunteered to go get Raider's mount. Things were moving. Raider's heart pounded inside his chest. He loved getting on to it so early in a case.

Inside Sheriff Daniels's office, they spread a map on the top of the desk. "Chaney's here," Daniels told him, pointing to a place west of Odessa. "Sharper is here, south of Chaney."

His black eyes committed the map to memory. "How close are they to the mountains?"

"Not too far. Mostly there's foothills there. A few ridges. No mesas, more like rollin' hills."

Raider looked up. He heard the snorting of his mount. He hoped the gray was ready to run again. It hadn't had much rest.

As he started toward the door, the sheriff stopped him. "If you ain't back by tomorrow mornin', I'm comin' after you, Pinkerton."

"I'll hold you t' that, Bit. In the meantime, you stick close by Chaney. This may be a trick t' draw me away, Injun-like."

"I will."

Raider hesitated. "You had any trouble with Injuns hereabouts?"

"No. Most of the Apache are up in New Mexico now."

"No stragglers, renegades?"

Daniels shook his head.

Raider hurried out to his gray. Only the gelding wasn't there. Chaney held the reins of a tall, black stallion. The animal had fire and fury in its dark eyes. It knew how to run and it would fly for the man who could handle it.

"The stable man had your saddle cleaned and ready," Chaney said. "He complained about being wakened, but I made it worth his while."

Raider saw his rifle and his saddlebags, both of which had been left with the livery man for safekeeping. "I cain't afford this animal, Chaney."

The old man's eyes were glowing white with life in the moonlight. "Raider, I had just about given up hope before you came. Now you seem to be on to something. It would mean a lot to me if you could find out who killed my family. Bring them to justice for me. Please."

He was almost moved by the sound of the old man's voice. But the eyes had him for a moment. He saw something there that had not been present in the old boy a few hours ago. Hope. The last grain for the man who had lost his family. Hope of discovery, of revenge. If nothing else, Chaney might get to see the killer swing at the end of a thick rope.

Raider took the reins of the black and swung into the saddle. "If I'm right about this, Mr. Chaney, it won't take long to end it."

Unless things went wrong, he thought to himself, which they sometimes did.

He spurred the black and drove west, away from the ghostly light of Odessa. The night had started to grow warm again. Clouds swept down from the north, swirling around the moon without really covering it. A good night to ride, to follow a trail.

He knew where John Sharper's place was located, but there

was no special reason to assume Sharper was heading there. Maybe the evidence he needed to destroy was at Chaney's place or somewhere else.

The trail jumped at him in the moonlight. Two riders, heading away from Sharper's hacienda. It had to be important for both of them to go so late. They were in a hurry, which meant they might make careless mistakes.

Raider spurred the black, driving west. The animal was a pleasure to ride: smooth power under him, blind speed. He had to slow every ten minutes to check the trail.

Sharper and his manservant were holding steady toward Sharper's place. According to the sheriff's map, they had not taken the road that would lead to Chaney's ranch. The rat ran back to his own hole most of the time.

Play it safe, he thought. Slow stalk on foot, watch them, see what turned up. There was no need to confront Sharper if the evidence was missing. Best to keep a distance until the dapper merchant produced the rope that would hang him high.

As he rode on through the warm wind, Raider wondered how one man could kill another for something as stupid as money. Sure, greed always called, but you didn't have to listen. No matter how much gold glittered, it was never shiny enough to make Raider pull the trigger on somebody, unless of course, that somebody was shooting at him first.

The hills began to rise higher around him. Small patches of trees rested atop some of the ridges, while others were bare and sandy.

Raider reined up, watching the trail. The tracks still bore in the direction of Sharper's country home. They were almost too easy to follow, the big man thought.

He kept riding, even though he had begun to wonder if the whole thing might be a trap.

The full moon brought them to life. They played between the sparse trunks of the trees, nipping and yapping, no threat to themselves.

They felt the hunger, but they waited for their two-legged companion to appear. Sometimes he brought the meat. Other times they hunted, feasting on two- or four-legged creatures. The two-legged one was their mother. Always. From the first eye opening, while they still suckled.

Like otters who needed no river, they swirled around each other in the currents of air; playful, frisky, no threat to the two figures that suddenly moved below them in the glow of the full moon. They stopped and ten sets of eyes watched the riders. Ears pricked at the wind. Maws closed tight. They stayed as still as rocks in the shadows. When the riders had passed, they remained motionless for a few moments.

The whistle came from behind them, alerting them to the arrival of the two-legged one. He had a fine, hairy face that they rubbed against. They bared their stomachs to him, surrendered to his superiority.

They didn't smell the meat which meant that they were going to hunt tonight.

The two-legged one began to lead them toward the riders, who looked over their shoulders when the howl went up over the rolling hills.

Raider guided the black to the top of the hill. He knew he was close to Sharper's place, so he figured to get a good look from the crest of the rise. There was still plenty of moonlight in the west. He could see the mountains in the distance. There was also an ill-defined box shape between him and the mountains. It must be Sharper's place, but it was dark.

Surely the merchant had been able to get there by now. The tracks were proof that they had come this way. Both mounts stayed together all of the way. So why hadn't they arrived yet at the dark house?

Raider dismounted and hunkered low, watching the place. If the lights came on, then Sharper and his man were there. If not, then they might be hiding somewhere on the trail, waiting for him.

The merchant was smart. He had probably known that Raider would come after him. It followed that an ambush would be in order. Studying the terrain from the top of the rise, Raider figured it would come from the stand of trees that lay between him and Sharper's place. It was a perfect bushwhacking spot.

The trees were slightly above the trail, providing cover for the ambusher.

So he waited, watching for signs of life from Sharper's house. There were no lights. No one arrived. Maybe they were just lying up there in the dark, waiting for him. Maybe Sharper had another pack of dogs to set on Raider.

He felt sweaty in the warm breeze. The canteen water tasted good.

He gave the black enough to wet his whistle. The animal pawed the earth, like it was ready to run. Raider patted his neck. "Soon enough, boy. Soon enough."

He turned his black eyes on the dark form of the house. Nobody was there. He felt it.

They were waiting for him.

What should he do? Circle back, get the sheriff, bring a posse. If there was a fight, he might be able to get Sharper with a stray bullet. Who could argue with the evidence then? As long as the merchant fired the first shot, Raider could plead self-defense.

The black snorted again. Raider gave a sharp pull on the reins. "Settle down, Jasper."

He gazed at the trail. Maybe he could decoy them. He could send the stallion riderless down the trail and draw their fire. He could then mark their positions and stalk them.

What if they sent dogs again? Then he would have to kill one of them and bring it back for evidence.

He had to laugh to himself at the thought of men turning into wolves. Had Sharper gone to great lengths to spread the rumor himself?

Raider hoped he could catch the man alive and red-handed. He wanted to talk to Sharper, to hear the plan firsthand.

The black lifted its feet, whinnying.

Raider jumped back, avoiding the hooves as they fell.

He was about to discipline the stallion, but then he heard it, too, faint and ominous on the breeze: The screams of men, a single gunshot, and then the echo of a shrill, wolf-like howling.

Their muzzles dipped into the blood. They had killed the riders because the two-legged one had willed it. They would have been just as content to kill the horses, but their master bade different. Fangs ripped at flesh.

The two-legged one had killed with them, finishing the riders after the attack. The gunfire had scared them, but the single shot had not been enough to frighten them away.

It was food, nothing more.

One or two of them looked back to see that the two-legged one was not feeding this time but their gullets needed filling, so they went back to the blood.

Suddenly the two-legged one was moving between them. He peered to the east.

Then their ears pricked and their eyes stared in the same direction. They all heard it, smelled it. Another rider was approaching, moving quickly.

The two-legged one stood there, deciding for them. Would they stay to face the intruder?

The two-legged one gave the signal and they started away, through the trees. A few were reluctant to leave the kill, but the two-legged one was there looking back at them. They knew they had to obey. He would kill one of the horses that had run away into the woods; but for now, they had to flee into the half-light of the evening.

As Raider approached the stand of trees, he reined the black. The stallion snorted, like it was afraid to go on. Raider dismounted. Something had gone wrong for Sharper and the Mexican. Maybe the manservant had used the dogs against his master. The screams still echoed in his ears. One of them—or both—had been in possession of a firearm. One shot. Had it been enough? Those damned screams.

Raider's hand rested on his Colt. He had to have a look, even if it meant a fight. He considered taking his rifle, but decided the Colt would be better at close range, even if he only had six shots. There was still no reason to be careless. He took the Winchester from the scabbard on his sling ring, placing the weapon carefully on the trail so he could run back to it if need be. An ace in the hole.

The black snorted again. Raider knew it could sense something ahead on the trail. Animals could smell danger—or blood.

He listened closely. Was that the wind in the trees or the sound of someone running away? He thought of the fox hiding behind the twig. It moved like a falling leaf and hid behind nothing.

He had to take a look; but before he went on, the big man from Arkansas decided to go back to get his rifle.

The trail narrowed a little. Raider held steady in the calm air. The wind could not penetrate the stand of trees, so the trail was quiet below. Shadows were all around him. The moon had sunk to the west, so the going was darker now.

He held his breath for a moment. Nothing. He picked up a rock and chunked it into the darkness in front of him. After the thud of the falling stone, the silence returned. He had hoped to draw fire from the trees, but there didn't seem to be anyone up there. Where the hell was Sharper? Raider almost wished for an ambush to chase the damned stillness away.

He felt like calling out, but decided to throw another stone that scared up nothing from the trees.

"Shit."

He kept moving on the trail, watching, listening. Maybe Sharper had decided to kill someone else out here.

Maybe—he felt the dead weight underfoot. Raider tripped over the bodies, tumbling headlong into the dust. He came up with his rifle, expecting them to set on him, but they didn't move. He hesitated, holding the rifle on them. "Okay, Sharper, it's over. You can quit playin' possum."

Nothing.

He bent to touch them, immediately feeling the blood. He didn't need the moonlight to know that they were both dead, with their throats ripped out.

The big man's bones went cold when he heard the howling. It reverberated from somewhere in the hills.

He watched the trees above him, but he could not see a thing.

More howling rose into the night.

He aimed the rifle at nothing, finally deciding not to shoot. No need to give his position away—unless the Wolfbrand already knew where he was.

Wolfbrand. He had thought it.

Striking a sulphur match, he held the flame close to what was left of the dead men's faces. He recognized Sharper's clothes and the other one was the Mexican.

"Son of a bitch."

Raider heard the howling again. He turned and broke into a run, hoping to find the source.

After he had gone a quarter mile on foot, the trail widened, opening onto the rolling plain. He peered to the west, where the last sliver of the moon rested on the rim of the mountains. For a moment, the horizon was still, motionless. Then he saw the shapes rising for a moment, going over a ridge as they headed toward the mountains. They were too far away for the rifle.

Raider shook his head, wondering if he could believe his eyes. A lone figure towered over the smaller shapes. It looked like a creature on two legs, running away with the other creatures yapping at his heels.

"Wolfbrand," Raider said. His skin crawled with a nasty chill. He told himself not to believe what he had seen. Just go get his horse, chase the killer, and hope that he could be a little more careful than Sharper had been.

The two-legged one led them back to the lair. There, he slit the throat of the horse, letting it die slowly so his family could feed. He would feed himself, after his children were finished.

The two-legged one was considering the danger he had felt from the big man on the trail. He had not counted on the big man. He would not be as easy to kill as the others had been.

Two of his children broke away from the body of the horse, fighting among themselves. He silenced them with a whistle.

Gradually, the others finished eating and the two-legged one bent to feed, to show them that he was theirs.

He had already decided to kill the tall man as soon as they got the chance. It had probably been a mistake to let him live on this moon-washed night, but he would have to die as soon as possible. The fangs of his children would silence the threat.

Raider lost their trail in the sandstone hills.

The black seemed to run faster when he turned the animal east again.

On the way back, he tried to find more signs of tracks. Some soft dirt or a patch of clay. Something to yield up what had killed the merchant and his servant. But the trail was too dry for good prints.

Raider had almost forgotten his brief glimpse of the shapes that had fled against the eerie horizon. It had probably been night birds anyway. Now that the sun rose with the first sign of morning, he found it easier to rationalize what he saw.

Still, there was no way to dismiss the bodies that waited for him back on the trail. Sharper and his valet were lying dead on the ground, blood caked and clotted all around them. The thick, sweet, hateful crimson had already begun to draw flies.

Raider dismounted and studied the corpses. His stomach turned, fighting him. But he had to stay professional, if nothing else. He would have to see what was there, decide what it really was, and find a way to kill it.

Their throats were gone. Most of their faces too. But that wasn't what he feared. He saw the tracks that had half-formed in the congealed blood.

The paw prints were clear in the blood. Round, padded toes, some trace of claws. Wolf tracks. For the Wolfbrand.

There was also a second set of tracks that was even more disconcerting. They seemed to belong to a man, at least the back half did. The heel of the print resembled a human, but the toes were clearly that of something else. The circles belonged to a padded foot, the same as the wolf tracks.

Wolfbrand.

Thank God the daylight had come. Raider didn't want to face the monster alone. He tried to shake off the chill, but it wouldn't leave his shoulders. He told himself that there wasn't a wolf-monster, even if he had begun to believe in it.

Raider hunkered in the shade, looking down at the bodies of the two dead men. He had found more wolf-sign in the trees; plenty of it. How the hell had Sheriff Daniels neglected to find the same thing? Maybe he hadn't looked so thoroughly, or maybe he was part of it.

What if a man could change himself into an animal? Indians in the north had always accepted the half-man called the Sasquatch. Every tribe had its own legends about monsters that came in the night. Most of them were based on visions and stories passed down around a campfire. Such tales were enhanced by loco weed or Indian brew.

Sharper and the Mexican had not been killed by a vision. Why the hell were they killed anyway? Maybe Sharper had been working with someone else, had paid the killer to do his dirty work. Raider had seen it before. The man with blood on his hands decides that he hasn't been paid enough and decides to kill his employer.

He found himself shuddering. He needed sleep, so he closed his eyes, cradling the Winchester to his chest like it was a beautiful woman.

In a half-waking dream, he saw the wolf coming straight at him. The teeth were white, bared, muzzle dripping with blood. The reverie startled him awake. He stood quickly and took a look at the sky. It was well past noon, he thought.

Birds flitted in the trees, singing their songs like the death below didn't bother them.

Raider stepped down the side of the hill, reaching for the canteen on the saddle of the black. The animal shook its head like it wanted to run. Raider drank from the canteen, which was almost empty. The water was warm and tasted like metal. He needed something cooler, wetter. The stallion needed to drink and eat.

He gazed back at the bodies again. What should he do?

He could take the corpses back to town, let the sheriff worry over them, and find someone to perform the burial. Sheriff Daniels would probably laugh at him, since Raider had been wrong about John Sharper. Of course, there was no way to discount Sharper's involvement until all the rocks had been turned over. The merchant's name had not yet been cleared, even with him lying dead at Raider's feet.

The big man from Arkansas sure didn't feel like doing the burying himself.

But he knew he had to do it. So he put them in shallow graves and covered them with dirt and rocks. By the time he had finished, the afternoon sun was sinking toward early evening.

He wiped the dirt from his hands, knowing where he had to go next. It was to Sharper's place. Maybe he could find some clues. He had to get back on track and pretend that he wasn't chasing a wolf-monster. He would try to hold steady; and he would make sure he had his Winchester handy at all times. The moon would soon be up again.

The big man from Arkansas wanted to finish his investigation so he could get back to Odessa before nightfall.

CHAPTER ELEVEN

The late John Sharper's cabin wasn't very fancy. Raider couldn't imagine why the dead merchant would have kept such a place. The land around it was poor and there wasn't any water, not even a deep well.

Raider searched the cabin, coming up empty. He did find a dog kennel in back, a shed made with wire and plank boards. But he already knew that Sharper had kept his dogs at this cabin. The merchant had confessed as much before the wolves got him.

The big man sat down in a wooden chair, trying to think. Maybe another set of dogs had gotten loose, attacking the two men who were coming to kill them. Of course, the kennel didn't show as many tracks as Raider had found in the trees above the trail. There must've been ten animals in that pack, while the sign at the kennel indicated no more than three hounds, the same number that Sharper had put to death in Odessa.

The facts still pointed to wrongdoing by the merchant. Hadn't he gone a long way toward ruining his competitor's life? Chaney's business was all but over. But then, so was Sharper's, when he thought about it.

He considered the tracks he had found. Definitely wolfen, unless there was some kind of dog he had never seen before.

Then there was the half-man, half-wolf track that he had found. It really wasn't too hard to answer, because the big man knew any kind of animal print could be faked. So he reasoned that a man was behind it all. But what kind of man could get a pack of wild animals to follow him? The Wolfbrand.

He got up and went through the cabin again.

Nothing. No real sign that anybody, much less John Sharper, had been there. It was almost like a line shack.

Someone could have cleaned the place out, to hide more evidence. Maybe the merchant and his manservant were heading back to check one more time, to make sure that there were no damning clues left behind. A final sweep to leave the bones picked clean for the big Pinkerton.

He returned to the wooden chair.

What next? Wasn't that always the question? You could wait, or you could stir something up, hope a big chunk floated to the top.

He got up and went onto the porch of the cabin.

The black was tied to a hitching post. It snorted a little, indicating that it was ready for a feed bag and some cool water. Raider figured the dinner hour was on him as well. He hadn't really eaten for a couple of days. A steak would have been good, with a mound of potatoes and onions.

His eyes scanned the surrounding landscape as twilight fell over the golden plain. He watched for signs of movement, for the flash of fur, a blurring dart of ear or snout. Something had attacked Sharper and the Chaney clan, and Raider was pretty sure it would come after him.

He patted the black on the neck. "You let me know if you smell somethin', boy. Don't be shy."

The black snorted again, impatiently awaiting its dinner. It wanted to be in the stable, safe from the approaching darkness. But Raider had no intention of going back to Odessa.

He knew he was close to the Chaney ranch. Even though it had been abandoned by its final residents, the place might give up some oats for the stallion and something for himself. It made sense to press on, especially when he was this close.

The black became unruly as Raider climbed into the saddle. He jerked the reins, turning the beast's head to the north. It was going to be a slow ride in the hills. There was no way to get back to Odessa before dark.

As he started forward, he hefted his Colt just to make sure it was loose and ready. The rifle butt was also within reach. Ten sets of tracks meant ten animals. That would call for some pretty quick shooting.

He had seen plenty of wolves, but not often in the southwestern regions. Washington, Montana, Idaho—those territories were lousy with wolves.

Of course, Texas wasn't devoid of the canine creatures. Raider had even been attacked once. He had managed to fend them off, but the attack had still scared the hell out of him.

The memory of the two-legged thing on the moonstruck horizon flashed before him.

What if a man could change into an animal? Sometimes there was Indian magic that just couldn't be explained away. Maybe it was some kind of Mescalero thing, a spell, a vision.

No, there had to be a real answer. Even if the Mescaleros could fool around with God's own creations, a man was a man and a wolf was a wolf. No such thing as in between, half and half.

The shadows grew longer as he rode on. To his left rose another wide, round moon.

A howling startled him into looking back over his shoulder. It took him a couple of moments to realize that a lone coyote was calling to the new shape in the sky. Coyotes weren't as bold as wolves. Raider had never known anyone to be attacked by a coyote.

He turned back and urged the stallion toward Chaney's place.

Sheriff Bit Daniels looked up when his office door opened. Jubal Chaney walked in, casting his strange eyes on the lawman. Daniels still wondered if a man with eyes like that was capable of killing his whole family. Maybe the Pinkerton would settle the whole thing for him.

"What can I do for you, Mr. Chaney?"

The older man sat down in a wooden chair. "The Pinkerton hasn't come back yet. I was wondering if you were going to look for him."

Daniels squirmed in his chair, remembering his promise to go after Raider if he wasn't back by morning. Another evening had already come on them and Daniels was still in his chair. Of course, Chaney hadn't heard the promise and Daniels figured it was the Pinkerton's case, anyway.

"That Pinkerton don't want me botherin' him," the sheriff offered. "And it's gettin' late. I got to make my rounds."

Chaney's face turned white. He leaned back, fanning himself with his hand. Daniels asked him if he wanted a glass of water.

"No, thank you," Chaney replied. "I want you to go look for Raider. If not tonight, then tomorrow."

Daniels leaned back, rubbing his nose. "Well, you did hire him and he's the one in charge of this."

Before Chaney could reply, a loud guffaw resounded from the cell room behind the sheriff. "Aw, you're just chicken-shit, sheriff. You're 'fraid that wolf is gonna git you."

The man named Red was still in lockup for his fight with Raider.

"Hush up, Red," the lawman called.

Red made a sound like a chicken clucking.

Daniels pointed a finger at him. "I mean it, Red. If you don't shut your yap, I ain't gonna give you no dinner."

That seemed to quiet him.

Chaney glared at the constable. "Maybe you are afraid, Daniels. Or maybe you don't want the Pinkerton to bring back the truth."

The lawman took offense. "Seems like you'd be the one who's afraid of the the truth, Chaney."

"Awrooo—"

Red had begun to howl like a wolf.

"Shut up!" the sheriff cried.

Chaney gestured toward the cell. "Why don't you let him out? You've had him in there for a whole day. Isn't that usually what men get for fighting?"

"I want to keep him there," Daniels replied. "Leastways till the Pink gets back. If Sharper did have somethin' to do with all your misery, then Red might be in on it, too."

"Sharper ain't done nothin'!" the prisoner cried.

"I told you to shut up, Red. One more blast and you ain't gonna have nothin' to eat tonight."

Chaney got up and started for the door.

"Chaney?"

"Yes, sheriff?"

Daniels sighed and leaned forward. "If the Pinkerton ain't back by tomorrow, I'll go lookin' for him."

Chaney nodded and left the office. Outside, he peered to the east, staring at the round orb that had begun to rise on the horizon. The full moon brought tears to his eyes. He cried for his lost family.

"Arooo—"

But it was only the prisoner mocking from his cell.

The sheriff called again, threatening to cancel dinner.

Chaney walked on toward his warehouse, crying as he went.

The creatures awoke with the full moon, the way others were roused by the morning sun. They went through their rituals as the group came to life. Sniffing, licking, mounting one another. The approach of the two-legged one snapped them back to obedience. They rubbed against his hairy snout, bared their bellies, felt the clawed hands on their stomachs. They did not challenge the two-legged one. He would slap down any who tried. He had sent them sprawling before when they flashed their teeth at him. Circling around him, they yapped for approval, hoping to feel the rough hand on their heads.

The two-legged one began to walk, to lead them down the slope. They retraced their steps, heading back to where they had killed the night before. The smell of death was fresh on the trail. One of them pawed at the earth where the bodies had been buried.

The two-legged one drew them together. He wanted them to trace another scent. The big man's smell was there, alongside the aroma of death. Immediately, the pack detected the trail. The tall man was riding a horse as well, so that scent was also there to lead them. The two-legged one followed them north, into the night.

They had to find the tall man; kill him, rip out his throat, and see his blood spreading in the light of the full moon.

CHAPTER TWELVE

William Wagner strode along the shore of Lake Michigan, gazing out at the reflection of the full moon on the water. There had long been a belief among the constables of Chicago that a full moon brought out the worst in people. The lunacy inflicted by the round, silver orb in the night sky had inspired husbands to grab carving knives and plunge them into the hearts of their wives. There were more brawls during a full moon, more thievery and pilferage.

Wagner himself took great comfort in the moon. He rarely strolled along the lake unless the moon was there to light the way. It was a pleasant diversion from the routine of the Pinkerton Agency, a chance to be alone after a hard day behind his desk. So it surprised and rather irked him to have his name called during his solitary walk along the shore.

"Mr. Wagner! Mr. Wagner!"

At first he had no recollection of the man's voice. As the caller drew closer, Wagner held his cane tightly, wondering if the intruder was someone who had suffered at the hands of the agency. Detectives made enemies even when they were serving the causes of righteousness.

"Mr. Wagner, I came all the way from the wire office."

It was the telegraph operator. The man had been known to range all over Chicago to bring Wagner important messages. On such occasions, the wires were usually from Stokes or Raider, Wagner's two troubleshooters.

"What is it now?" Wagner asked rather irritably.

"From Stokes." The man held out the message. "I think he's in trouble, Mr. Wagner."

Wagner read the wire. "Drat! They've arrested him."

"Want to send back a reply?"

"No, I need to think on this until morning. What time will you open the key tomorrow?"

"Six A.M., as usual."

Wagner reached into his pocket, but found that he had no form of currency to render the man a gratuity. "I'm afraid I'm—"

"Hey, you don't have to do that, sir. It makes me feel good just to bring you these telegrams. Kind of like I'm doin' somethin' good, 'stead of just workin' a key. Know what I mean, Mr. Wagner? You must feel like that sometimes, directin' all your men."

Wagner gave him a blank look. "Drop 'round the office tomorrow and I'll give you fifty cents."

"Fifty cents?" He sounded disappointed.

"All right," Wagner replied defeatedly, "one dollar."

"Thank you, sir. Thanks a lot." He left Wagner to muse in silence.

Stokes was in trouble. Who would he send? He knew there was really only one choice: Raider. But it might take a year to find him in Texas.

Wagner looked back at the full moon, cursing it for his bad luck, unaware of the trouble it was bringing to the big man from Arkansas. He turned back toward the office, walking a little faster. He wished he had more men like Stokes and Raider. They were the last of a breed. Wagner wondered how long it would be before the full moon claimed them both.

CHAPTER THIRTEEN

The black stallion was loping toward the horizon when Raider saw the Chaney place in front of him. He slowed the stallion to a walk, trying to stay alert in the first eerie glow of the moon. Something told him that he would hear the threat before he saw it. The shadows were too deep for him to be able to see them coming. The animals had an advantage; whether they were hounds or wolves, they could see in the dark.

Damn, it had to be dogs. Wolves couldn't be mastered. The most experienced trapper couldn't snare a whole pack of them.

The black held steady, making for the house. Why had he stayed out past dark? A tightness spread over his shoulders. Raider tried to shake it off. He had never been afraid to tackle any mystery; or even if he had been scared, he had never let it stop him.

Something howled behind him. It didn't sound like coyotes.

He spurred the black again, loping toward the shadowed house in the distance.

• • •

Chaney's house was something of a payoff.

Sitting on the back porch, munching on a hunk of smoked meat, Raider had to feel a little better about things. He had found plenty to eat, that which the raccoons hadn't been able to find. There had also been some stale oats and hay for the stallion. Chaney even had a pump, with cool water flowing from the ground.

There was something else, too: A five-pointed star had been painted on the floor of the kitchen. Raider had seen it when he lit the oil lamp to look for food. It was the sign of the Wolfbrand.

Why hadn't he found the same sign by the bodies of Sharper and his valet?

Maybe he had scared off the assailants. They had probably heard him coming. That close! He just wanted one rifle shot to find out if the Wolfbrand knew how to bleed.

He gazed out toward the stable area. Chaney had constructed a pretty nice barn with a big corral. It must have cost a fortune to haul out all that wood from Odessa. He probably had to wait months for it to be shipped in. There wasn't much timber, not the logging kind, in west Texas. Just a few stands of cottonwood or pine.

Chaney must have really loved his family. The house was big enough for a whole crew of men. It was fancier than the cabin Sharper had built.

Sharper's cabin was too sparse, Raider thought. Sharper had come out to keep tabs on Chaney. The cabin was a look out post, a base for operating in the same territory. Sharper hadn't really lived there. His hired man had probably done the spying.

Down at the stable, the black whinnied.

Raider drew his Colt and moved slowly toward the stallion. Maybe this was it. His rifle was on the saddle in the barn.

The livery area was dark.

Raider didn't have to find the stallion. The black wandered over from the corral, no doubt looking for another helping of oats.

"Look at you. Next thing you know, you'll be actin' like a New Orleans carriage pony. Just eat, sleep, and go 'round t' the gamin' houses on the weekends." He piled some hay in the corral.

When he turned back toward the house, he felt his heart acting up again. It was the light from the oil lamp he had lighted. For a moment, he thought the light was something else. But what? The glowing eyes of an animal. He decided to get his rifle.

Raider wondered if the stable man had kept a bottle when the place was full of life. Maybe behind one of the rafters. If there was a— His fingers hit a glass bottle. He popped the cork and sniffed the liquor. It smelled a lot like whiskey, although it could have been liniment. He touched some of it to his tongue. The burn was there. He could always rub it on the stallion if it didn't go down right.

Luckily, it didn't taste as bad as it smelled. He drank a few swallows and leaned back against the wall of a stall. Maybe the hooch would help him think.

Sharper was dead. That meant someone had double-crossed him—if Sharper was involved. But who?

He thought about Chaney's wife, standing in the kitchen.

Where had the animal come from?

Raider went outside and gazed toward the corral. The black stallion had gone to the water trough.

He imagined one animal, moving slowly, coming up through the corral. It probably spooked some horses, so maybe the woman looked out the window. What the hell was she doing alone? Everybody was searching for the animal that had killed her sons.

He had seen the throats for himself. How the hell could somebody get a dog to be so vicious? Growing up in Arkansas, Raider had heard that you could make a dog meaner by feeding it gunpowder. He had never believed that, but now it made him wonder. Had somebody really instilled a hound with the instinct to hunt and to kill human beings?

The stallion raised its head from the water trough. Raider peered at the horse. "Whatta you want?"

A snort from the brawny steed. Then it pawed the dirt.

Raider gazed toward the back of the corral, but saw nothing in the moonglow.

The stallion began to dance, snorting, kicking at the air. Dust rose beneath its feet.

"What the hell is it, Jasper?"

Rearing, the stallion struck the air in front of it.

Raider looked over his shoulder, toward the house. The lamp still burned in the kitchen. Orange light spilled against the walls.

Raider held his breath. Someone was moving around in Chaney's kitchen. A silhouette had been cast against the wall. Then a face appeared at the back window, easing up to look out toward the corral.

Raider clicked a cartridge into the chamber of the Winchester and started toward the house.

CHAPTER FOURTEEN

Raider tried to stay low. He didn't want the glowing eyes to see him. The face still hovered at the window, awash in the light of the oil lamp. What the hell was there inside Jubal Chaney's kitchen? The head looked to be round, like the head of a man. Then the head disappeared.

Raider hoped like hell that the intruder hadn't seen him.

There were more shadows on the wall. Whatever was in there had started to move.

The back door swung open before he got there. The intruder had definitely seen him. A small, dark shape burst out of the house, running to his right, trying to escape.

Raider fired one shot, but the intruder was too fast. He broke into a run, chasing after the figure.

It ran like a man. Only it was smaller, too quick for him. Like chasing a ferret through a maze of fallen logs. The shape headed toward the corral, at least until Raider let another slug fly from the rifle. That turned the interloper toward the stable. Raider was right behind it, puffing in the shadows.

He hesitated at the entrance, listening to the sounds of the night.

Something scratched in front of him.

Raider fired a quick burst.

A painful squeal rose through the barn.

He struck a match to see that he had cut a barn rat into two pieces.

The match burned his fingers.

He wanted to curse.

Something creaked in the rafters of the loft.

Raider jacked another shell into the Winchester. "You got about five seconds t' come on down here."

No more sounds came from above.

Raider didn't want to go up after it. "I mean it. If you ain't down here on the count o' five, I'm gonna start shootin' up the place. Chaney won't care if there's a few bullet holes in his barn."

Nothing.

"One—"

He held the rifle up to his shoulder, taking aim.

"Two—"

Raider heard more creaking. For a moment, he thought the intruder was going to surrender but instead, a dark figure flew from the loft, landing on a moldy haystack behind the barn. Raider fired the Winchester again but he was certain that he had not hit a thing. The shape was off and running again, heading for the back of the corral.

Raider went to the front of the wooden railing, gazing into the shadows. Suddenly the shape burst into the moonlight, sliding through the railing, making for the strong back of the stallion. He raised the rifle, but the figure cut between him and the horse.

"Damn."

It knew how to ride. It vaulted through the air, landing on the horse's back. The stallion reared, striking out with his front legs.

Raider went over the fence, taking the rifle with him. He could see the intruder fighting the stallion, holding on to the mane. Did it really think it would be able to ride the black to freedom?

He took aim again, but the stallion had started to buck.

The interloper couldn't hang on.

It flew through the eerie night, landing with a splash in the watering trough. The stallion wasn't finished. He tried to kill the thing with his hooves. Raider had to step in to stop him.

"Good work, boy, now back off."

The stallion strutted away, shaking its head.

"Yeah, you're a real stud. This thing ain't even ten times smaller'n you or nothin'."

He reached for the wet lump in the trough. It felt like some sort of hide, like buckskin. Was it still alive? He decided to have a look in the light of the kitchen. Grabbing a handful of the strange hide, he pulled the lump out of the trough and started to drag it to the house.

The lump began to wriggle as he hefted it up the steps. It was still alive.

At least he'd have a good look now.

He put the thing in the center of the kitchen and held the lamp over it.

The big man's eyes widened when the bundle unfolded to reveal the soft, angular face of an Apache woman. She had long black hair and wore a buckskin dress. Her eyes turned up, flashing at Raider.

"Well, you ain't no wolf."

She tried to move toward the door.

He showed her the barrel of the Winchester. "Nope, you ain't a wolf at all. And lookin' at that face, I sure as hell know you ain't no dog."

When she looked away, he lifted the rifle and asked her if she spoke the white man's tongue.

They were getting closer, anticipating the taste of blood. The two-legged one was there beside them, directing the way.

They stopped dead still when the shots erupted from the house in the distance. The two-legged one peered toward the dwelling. He knew they would have to be careful. The big man could shoot.

They curled around his legs. Hunger had taken hold of them. They were used to feasting each night. Still, they could feel the concern of the two-legged one, so they took their cue from the leader.

The leader knew that the big man had to be killed. He wasn't like the fat sheriff in Odessa. He would keep coming until he was dead, so he had to die. It was the only way to end it.

They yipped at the moon. The two-legged one made a hand gesture that told them to be quiet. There would be no howling this night, just blood to wet their fangs, dripping from their maws, quenching the ancient thirst deep within them.

Raider stared down at the beautiful face. She would not look at him. A tiny thing, although she was old enough to have curves beneath the buckskin. She was more woman than girl, and was so scared she was trembling.

"I asked if you spoke the tongue of the white man."

She finally nodded, looking at the floor.

"Say somethin'."

Her eyes lifted. "What would you have me say?"

He leaned back against the door, still holding the rifle at ready. "Speak English pretty good. Some Bible thumper get a hold of you?"

"I learned at the mission."

He studied her in the orange glow. Her skin was lighter than most Apaches. There were streaks of brown in her hair. Her eyes had a funny discoloration in the middle of the dark irises; flecks of white.

"Don't look at me like that,"she said.

He ignored her. "Honey, why ain't you up in New Mexico with the rest o' the Apache?"

She looked at the floor again.

He didn't press her. Indians could be just as proud as anyone else. If the girl wasn't with her tribe, then it probably meant that she had been turned out for some reason. A disgrace. Otherwise, a young buck would have jumped at the chance to marry this beautiful squaw.

"You come here lookin' for food?"

She nodded.

He told her where to find the smoked meat. There was even a can of peaches that he had planned to take with him, but she could have it now.

She ate like it was her last meal. Raider opened the can for her. She slurped the peaches straight from the tin.

"Didn't they teach you no table manners at that mission?"

Her face scowled her rage at him.

"Whoa, lady, you don't have to look at me like that. I'd be happy t' let you go if you'd answer a few questions for me."

The strange eyes seemed to soften. "Questions?"

Raider exhaled. "Goin's on in this part o' Texas. Killin's. Some say it's a animal that's half man, half wolf. The Wolfbrand."

"Madre Dios!" She crossed herself, a sign of her training at the mission. "Do not speak of such things."

"Why? Because the moon is full?"

"No," she replied, "the Wolfbrand can appear any time. I have heard the stories. My people have a great chief, Walking Eagle. He is a medicine man. Some say he conjured the Wolfbrand."

Raider pointed to the star shape on the floor. "That mean anything to you? The star."

She shook her head. "I have never seen it before."

He frowned. "No?"

"Never."

He took a deep breath, wondering what to do with her. "Your people send you packin'?" he asked finally.

She looked sideways at him. "No."

"Then you're just out here wanderin' 'round in the wilderness?"

She looked away. "Christ Our Lord spent much time in the wilderness. He was better for it."

"Walkin' Eagle send you away after you went with the priests?"

"No, it was—"

He finished the sentence for her. "Afore you went with the priests? Is that it?"

A single tear began to roll down her cheek. He couldn't remember ever seeing an Apache cry. Maybe she had learned that in the mission.

"Why'd he send you away?"

"I won't tell you," she replied. "Why are you torturing me like this?"

He shrugged. "I don't know. Mebbe I think you know somethin' 'bout all this Wolfbrand business. Mebbe you can tell me 'bout Walkin' Eagle. Is he in the middle of all this?"

She filled her mouth with peaches.

Raider figured he had one last card to play. "Well, if that's the way you want it, reckon I got no choice but t' take you t' the nearest Indian agent. Maybe he'll—"

"No!"

That got her. She turned to look at him. Raider felt sort of sorry for her when he saw the desperation in her flecked eyes.

"Honey, what else can I do? I cain't leave you to roam 'round out here like a animal. Hell, that thing done kilt two men last night. Who knows how many more it'll kill tonight?"

More tears. "I don't know anything of the Wolfbrand. I only came looking for my brother. He left the reservation and I want to find him."

"You were at the reservation?" he asked.

"No, at the mission. But I heard of his leaving, so I came to look for him. I want to find him so we can be together."

Raider was going to ask her brother's name, but he never got the words out of his mouth. The stallion began to whinny and cry.

The girl saw the look in his eyes. "What is it?"

He peered through window to see the stallion bucking again.

She stepped up beside him. "What do you—"

"Shh!"

He watched and listened. The stallion wasn't going crazy for nothing. It had seen or heard something.

Shadows flitted in front of the big man's eyes.

Was that something moving in the darkness?

Several shapes darted back and forth.

They were stalking him.

Why hadn't they gone after the stallion if they were hungry?

The girl gasped. She had seen them, too. Had the whole pack come to kill him?

A dark form flew through the air, coming straight for the window.

Raider grabbed the girl and pushed her out of the way.

The animal crashed through the panes of glass, landing in the middle of the kitchen table. Raider lifted the Winchester and immediately fired two shots into the creature. It fell to the kitchen floor, writhing on the shape of the unholy star. He shot it again, just to make sure it was dead.

The girl began to scream.

Raider grabbed her and lifted her to her feet.

He could hear the others outside, circling the back porch like a school of hungry fish.

He fired the rifle through the window, scaring them back, shooting until the last cartridge was gone.

"We gotta get outta here," he told the girl.

She nodded, holding his hand.

"Get on my back," he said, "like a piggyback ride."

"What are you going to do?"

"We're leavin', honey."

"No!"

"Not through the back door," he said, kneeling. "Just climb on if you wanna stay alive."

She got onto his back.

Raider immediately grabbed the oil lamp and dashed it against the wall of the house. The flames started to rise toward the ceiling. He knew the fire would keep them back, at least until he escaped through the front.

He stepped over the dead animal, wishing that he had time to take a closer look. It appeared to be a wolf, but he couldn't be sure. He had to run for now, to get away with his life. The weight of the girl was no burden as he moved toward the front of the house.

Jubal Chaney wasn't going to like the fact that Raider had burned his place down, but that didn't seem to matter much at the moment.

When he crashed through the front door, Raider saw the two-legged figure staring at him. It had a wolf face but stood erect like a man. He fired a single shot but the creature was already gone.

Raider figured to do the same himself. He started running toward the corral. They could take the stallion, ride him bareback, go get help.

The girl cried out again.

Raider knew why she was shrieking. He heard the animals behind him. They had turned away from the fire to give chase.

He drew his Colt, shooting as he ran, hoping the bursts from the gun would hold them back. He heard yelping. Another one fell into the dirt, squirming from the bullet wound.

Raider vaulted the corral fence, running toward the stallion. The horse was skittish but he managed to catch hold of its neck.

Even as he swung onto the bare back, carrying the girl with him, the creatures at the rail began to circle again.

At least the stallion was ready to run.

Raider urged it toward the fence. For a moment, he thought the black was going to crash into the corral. But instead, the stallion gave a strong, beautiful leap that carried them over the top rail. He almost fell off when the animal hit the ground.

Even as it ran, the pack charged one last time. They were quick, nipping at the hamstrings on the horse's back legs. The stallion missed a step, which made Raider believe that one of the wolfish maws had found its mark, but the stallion was too fast. It outran the pack in a hurry. The hot Texas air rushed by them as they escaped. Raider wished he hadn't left his saddlebags behind, but as it stood, he thanked providence that he had at least been able to get away with his life.

The pack was no longer whole. The big man's guns had killed two of them. They whimpered at the sight of the dead one, nudging the body with their noses.

Turning toward the house, several of them watched as the two-legged one doused the flames set by the man with the guns.

When the fire was out, the two-legged one carried the body of his child from the house. He laid it next to the body of the second animal. Cries of anguish came from his pointed snout. He thrashed the ground, causing his children to back away from him. They would keep their distance until the two-legged one buried the corpses of their kin. Then they would go after the big man again, to avenge the death of their brothers, blood for blood, as long as the two-legged one was there to lead them into battle.

Raider kept the stallion at a full run. He still could not believe what he had seen. Those were wolves attacking. But that wasn't what threw him. He kept wondering if he had really seen the creature on two legs, the half-man with the wolf face. It could have been a mask, he told himself. It could have been the Wolf-brand.

Just keep the stallion steady. Make for town. He wished like hell that he had been able to get his saddlebags, but it was all right for now—at least until the stallion went lame.

The mount began to stumble about a half hour after they left Chaney's place. When Raider felt the back leg give, he knew that one of the wolves had taken a hunk out of the black's hock. Sure enough, when he stopped to have a look, he saw blood there.

The girl stood beside him, holding on for dear life. "Is he going to die?"

"No," Raider replied, "but he ain't gonna run, neither."

He looked up, trying to take his bearings. "I think we're somewhere near Sharper's old place."

"Where?"

"There's a cabin out here, a line shack," he replied.

She started forward. "I know where it is. I passed it coming this way. I can find it."

Raider started to protest, but then he reasoned that an Apache, even a squaw, had a better sense of direction in the dark. He let her lead the way, pulling the lame animal behind him. He could always feed it to the wolves if they came back. The thought raised the hair on the back of his neck. The full moon sank steadily toward the mountains in the west. It was going to be a hell of a long night.

"There it is," the girl said.

Raider could see the shape of the cabin. It seemed peaceful enough. He waited for a while, making her wait with him.

"We'll be safe there," she said.

"Mebbe. Tell you what. You go on down there an' see if it's clear. I'll wait here for you."

That kept her quiet.

Raider finally figured they had better take shelter for the rest of the night. Even if the animals returned, they'd still have a better chance inside. As they moved toward the dark dwelling, he wished he had more cartridges than those on his gun belt. He could fill his Colt again, but the rifle was going to stay empty for a while.

The cabin door was wide open.

Raider looked at the Apache woman. "You been through here?"

"Yes, but I didn't find anything."

"Neither did I, honey, neither did I."

He reloaded the Colt and moved slowly through the door. There was nothing inside. It was the same way he had left it. The girl couldn't have been too far behind him the whole way. Had she been following him deliberately?

"It's okay," he told her.

She moved in beside him. "I hate this place."

"I ain't too wild 'bout it myself, woman."

"My name is Yellow Fox," she told him indignantly.

Raider exhaled and leaned his rifle against the wall. "Glad t' know you, Yellow Fox." He sat down next to his Winchester.

She sat down not too far from him. "What's your name?"

"Raider."

She shivered. "Wolves. Why were they after you?"

Raider squinted at her. He could barely see her face in the dimness. He asked her what she had seen at the Chaney place.

"Wolves," she repeated. "You saw them."

"Just wanted t' know what you saw," he offered. "How 'bout the one on two legs. You see him?"

She put a hand to her throat. "I don't know."

"You saw him. So did I. I woulda shot him, but he was too quick."

Yellow Fox slid closer to him. "The Wolfbrand. Walking Eagle gave him the power to change into a wolf."

"Coulda been wearin' a mask."

"No," she said emphatically, "I looked at his hands. He had claws. It was a wolf in the shape of a man."

Raider dropped his Colt in his lap. "I reckon it was. Damn, they really came after me. If the stallion hadn't been so fast, we never woulda got away."

Yellow Fox glanced toward the door. Raider had tied the lame horse close to the doorway, so the animal's whinnying would alert them to new dangers outside. She asked if Raider was going to shoot the animal. He replied that he wanted to take the stallion back to Odessa, to return it to the stable.

"I hope they don't have to shoot him," the girl said.

Raider put his arm around her shoulder. "I hope that myself, Yellow Fox. I surely do."

She slid beside him, putting her head on his chest.

In a few minutes, they were both asleep.

Raider kept waking each time the horse moved outside.

He half expected to see the wolves attacking again.

How many had he killed?

Two of them?

And what about the one who walked like a man?

If they made it back to Odessa, he'd have to get a posse up. Maybe even alert the army. What were they all going to say when he told them that he had discovered proof of a man-wolf?

Pinkerton and Wagner would have to be told. They probably wouldn't laugh, as they had read countless reports of similar adventures. Only this time, Raider had to wonder if he would ever get to the bottom of this one.

The girl stirred on his chest. "What is it?"

"Nothin'."

A howling rose outside.

Yellow Fox tensed. "Is that—"

"Just a coyote," he told her. "Listen, the stallion is quiet. He won't get nervous unless somethin' comes close."

She fussed for a while but then she drifted back to sleep. She felt safer with the big man beside her.

Who the hell would make him feel safe?

He had to get back to Odessa somehow. Maybe he'd find the stray horse that Sharper had been riding, or the black might be able to run again in the morning.

His hand closed around the butt of the Colt. His eyes got heavier.

The big man from Arkansas fell into a dream, running from a pack of wolves that all ran on two legs. They were fast, but he always managed to wake up again before they caught him.

CHAPTER FIFTEEN

Raider opened his eyes, trying to figure out what was different. The cabin was aglow with the first light of day. A warm breeze stirred the morning air.

The Indian girl had straddled him. Yellow Fox's fingers stroked the rigid timber that protruded from his fly. It was a pleasant change from the wolf dream. But he wasn't sure he should let it go on.

"Honey, I—"

She put a finger to his lips. "Let me. Please."

"But—"

She lifted her buckskin dress. Raider saw the dark patch between her thighs. She guided the head of his prick toward the entrance of her vagina. He didn't have the resolve or the inclination to stop her. Yellow Fox closed her eyes.

He felt the moistness between her legs. Sometimes danger could get women excited; and they had slept together all night.

She jerked him, gradually accepting a few inches of his cock. Yellow Fox gasped. "You're so big."

"If it's too much—"

But it wasn't. His cock disappeared inside her. She began to move her hips up and down, taking him along with her. Raider leaned back, enjoying the ride.

She wasn't a cherry. She had done this before. She had probably had a husband at some point.

Her face wrinkled as she found her pleasure. She collapsed on top of him, kissing his face.

Raider wasn't finished yet. His manhood ached for the same release. He was aroused enough to forget the danger that had plagued them the night before. His hands cupped her ass. It was tight and round. He felt the soft skin for a few moments before he started to move.

Yellow Fox knew what he wanted. They wrestled for a few seconds until Raider was on top. She peered up at him with those white-flecked eyes. "Yes," she moaned. "Yes." She also muttered something in Apache.

Raider didn't care what she was saying. He began to drive his prick in and out of her. Yellow Fox lifted her legs a little. She started toward the verge of another climax.

Yellow Fox cried out when she felt the expanding rush of Raider's cock. He buckled, driving it deep inside her, releasing with the desperation of a man who had been through hell the night before.

When he rolled off her, he stared up at the ceiling of the cabin. "That felt pretty good, honey."

Yellow Fox sighed. "When I woke up next to you, I thought of my husband. I wanted it then."

"Where is he?"

"Dead."

Raider didn't ask for details, but the woman supplied them anyway. Smallpox had taken her man. He wasn't an Apache. She had married a Mexican man she met at the mission. She missed him a lot.

"So that's why you come lookin' for your brother? 'Cause you ain't got no other kin left?"

She nodded. "And I will never marry again. Who would want me? My own people made me leave the reservation."

"Why?"

A deep sigh from her dainty chest. "It was said that my father was a white man. But I don't know if it's true."

Raider figured she might be a half-breed. Her skin was lighter than most Apaches. The yellowish tone, which resembled the color of an Oriental, had probably been the reason for her name.

"I hope you find your brother," Raider offered.

She sighed and began to rub his chest. Gradually her hand worked its way down to his groin. She touched his prick, which still protruded from his jeans. Raider immediately sprang to life.

"Don't start nothin' you cain't finish," he told her, but she was completely ready to finish him.

He didn't want to think of all the things that needed doing.

"Take off the rest of your clothes," he told her.

Yellow Fox stood up and obeyed him.

She was smaller than he liked them, but everything was there. The priests at the mission had been feeding her. When she climbed on top of him, he put his lips around the tiny brown bud of her nipple.

She started to breathe heavily. Her hips rotated, working the mound of hair against his cock. He rolled her over before she could get it inside her.

"You're a pretty little thing."

"Just do it," she told him.

Raider prodded her until he felt the soft folds give way. His prick sank to the hilt. Yellow Fox gasped and began to move her hips. They buckled the floorboards until Raider shot again.

He climbed off, thinking that he had no right to feel so good; not with the way the investigation had been going.

Yellow Fox scampered about, putting on her clothes. "I'm hungry," she told him. "We need food."

Raider stood, hitching up his pants, buttoning the fly. "Quickest thing we need to do is get back to Odessa."

She frowned. "I can't go there."

"Why?"

"There's an Indian agent in Odessa," she replied. "He'll try to send me back to the reservation."

Raider put his hands on her shoulders. "Mebbe that'd be best, honey. Your brother'll probably turn up sooner or later."

"No, he won't."

He looked into her pretty eyes. "Now you cain't be sure o' that. You never know when he'll come lookin' for you."

A dour expression came over her countenance. She put her face on his chest and began to cry. Raider held her, assuring her that she would be all right. He'd help her get back to the reservation, if that was what she wanted.

"You don't understand," she went on, "I have to find him. If I don't, there will be great trouble."

Before he could offer further consolation, the stallion snorted outside, bringing him back to the matters at hand.

"At least the horse is still alive," the big man said.

He broke away from the girl, reaching for his Colt.

"Don't leave me," she begged.

"Just goin' t' have a look."

"Hurry."

The black shook its head when Raider walked out of the cabin. He was ready for his morning oats. Not feeling too badly for a mount that had been bitten the previous night.

Raider patted the animal's neck. "You'll be okay, Dobbin. Let's have a look at that hock."

Yellow Fox emerged from the cabin to help him. "Is he hurt bad?"

Raider knelt to look at the wound. "Well, he's gonna favor it for a while. Don't reckon we'll have to shoot him, but it looks like we might have to walk back to—"

The stallion snorted again, pawing the earth with his front foot.

"What is it, boy?"

Yellow Fox peered toward the hills. "Somebody's coming."

Somebody or some*thing*, the big man thought.

Would those wolves return in broad daylight?

He was still holding the Colt. He waved the gun, telling Yellow Fox to get inside. He didn't have to tell her twice.

When the girl was hidden, he spun the cylinder of the Colt. All six shots were in place. As he moved toward the intruder, he wished that he had cartridges for the Winchester.

The Colt would just have to be enough.

• • •

Raider's heart pounded a hole in his chest as he lay in wait for the approaching rider.

The two clumps of sage were barely enough cover, but it had to do.

He had been able to catch sight of the man only once. The rider was studying the trail, looking for clues. Now he was almost on top of Raider. It was then that the big man saw the lawman's badge glinting in the sun.

He waited until the rider had passed him.

Then he rose, stepping out behind the sheriff. "Lookin' for me, Daniels?"

A startled lawman turned to look at him. "Pinkerton?"

Raider holstered the Colt. "Yep."

Daniels glared at him. "Where the devil have you been, Raider?"

The big man shrugged. "Runnin' from wolves."

"Come again?"

Raider gestured toward the cabin. "I'll tell you all about it. But there's somebody I want you t' meet."

The sheriff squinted at him. "Dog me if you don't look a mess, Raider. You find trouble?"

"More than I bargained for, Bit."

Daniels dismounted. "You know anything about them two bodies that was buried back yonder in that stand of trees?"

Raider nodded. "Yeah, I know all about 'em. How the hell did you find 'em, anyways?"

The sheriff seemed to take offense. "I ain't blind, Pinkerton. I saw the blood. I saw where somebody had dragged 'em up into the bushes there. Didn't bury 'em too deep."

"You recognize 'em?"

Daniels tipped back his hat. "Looked to be Sharper and the Mex."

"None other."

The lawman took off his hat and wiped his face with the back of his hand. The summer heat was already making him sweat. He looked like he needed a stiff shot of red-eye.

"They was ripped up like Chaney's clan," the sheriff went on. "Like animals got a hold of 'em."

Raider took a deep breath. "Yeah, that's it, Daniels. Just like the others. Only I saw the killers for myself."

The lawman's eyes grew wide. "The hell you say!"

"Wolves," Raider went on. "Leastways as far I as I could tell. Didn't hang around long enough t' get a real good look. I even managed t' shoot one of 'em. I think I killed it."

Daniels gazed toward Sharper's cabin. "Happen there?"

"No, I was over at Chaney's place."

The lawman peered in the opposite direction. "And you saw Sharper and his man get it?"

"No, I was a little late for that one. But I caught sight of them that did it. They was runnin' away toward the mountains."

Daniels seemed doubtful, but he motioned toward the cabin. "Let's get out of this sun."

He started toward the cabin.

Raider fell in beside him. "Yep, I got me another witness. Indian girl. Claims she's lookin' for her brother who left the Apache reservation."

"We'll see," the sheriff replied.

"I hope you brought some whiskey," Raider offered.

"In my saddlebag, but we're gonna wait a while."

Daniels gawked at the stallion when he saw it tied in front of the cabin. "That mount looks like it's been through hell."

"We all have," Raider replied. "Yellow Fox! Girl!"

He stuck his head in the cabin and called for her again.

"I'm waitin' for her," the sheriff said skeptically.

"She musta saw your star, Daniels. She ran off 'cause she's afraid you're gonna give her up to the Indian agent."

The lawman eyed him. "Looks like your story ain't holdin' too much water, Pinkerton. I need proof."

Raider pointed to the black. "Take a look at the stallion's back leg. Got bit pretty bad."

Daniels studied the wound on the animal's leg. "Yeah, that could be a bite. Where's the saddle and your gear?"

"At Chaney's place."

"You just left it?"

Raider told him how the wolves had ambushed them.

"That quick?" the sheriff asked.

The big man from Arkansas began to steam a little. "You saw

what happened to Sharper. I was in a hurry to clear the place before I ended up like him."

"That could be. But the way I see it, Pinkerton, when you left Odessa, you were dead set on pinnin' this thing to Sharper's chest. How do I know you didn't kill him and then make it look like all this happened?"

"I ain't that stupid, sheriff."

"Then you tell me that you've got a Apache girl with you, only she ain't nowhere to be seen."

Raider pointed a finger at the lawman. "Now look here, Daniels. I done rode through the night, been chased by wolves, an' now the only witness I got has run away b'cause you wore your badge out here. I ain't in no mood for pussyfootin' on this thing."

"I need more proof, Pinkerton."

"Then prove this, lawman. One of them wolves was on two feet. You hear me. I seen it twice. First it was runnin' away with the others. Then it was standin' outside at Chaney's place."

"The Wolfbrand?"

"You want proof, we gotta go to Chaney's."

The sheriff glanced at the black. "That stallion don't look like he's goin' anywhere too soon."

Raider said they could ride double. The sheriff didn't like the idea of sharing his mount, but the big man from Arkansas didn't care much about what the sheriff did or didn't like. He had something to prove. Even if he wasn't sure he believed it himself.

It was a stormy morning at the Pinkerton National Detective Agency's offices. Wagner had been in a gloomy mood. So far no word of Raider had turned up.

Wagner glared at the telegraph operator who sauntered into the office just after eight o'clock. "Well?" Wagner asked in a huffy tone.

"I sent those telegrams to Odessa," the man replied. "Just like you asked."

"Any reply?" Wagner was awfully close to losing his temper. "Well, speak up, man! Any word from Raider?"

"No reply, sir. It's just—the dollar, from last night. You promised a dollar and—"

Wagner gave him the money to get rid of him.

"Damn it all," he said aloud.

He remembered the first days of his employment at the agency, before the wire had stretched into the smaller towns west of the Mississippi. Wagner had been pleased when the telegraph became a more useful tool. But now it didn't seem fast enough. Why couldn't they come up with something better?

He looked at his desk but he could not concentrate.

Stokes was still in trouble. He had sent a man to monitor the affair, but the agent wasn't up to snuff, not if action had to be taken. Raider was the one he needed. Of course, the big galoot was probably in trouble himself.

Wagner could do very little but fume. And even when he got a reply from Texas, it wouldn't be the one he wanted.

Sheriff Daniels didn't like riding double, but he seemed convinced that they had to have a look at the Chaney place.

His mount was a chestnut gelding, not fast but steady. It resisted the weight of two men at first, before it gave in and plodded to the north. The way wasn't as far in the daytime.

"This better be good," Daniels said.

Raider told him to be patient. "I'll solve this thing if you'll just let me, Bit."

"That's what you been sayin' all along, Pinkerton, only the same nonsense keeps poppin' up."

"Trust me," was Raider's only reply.

When they reined up in front of the Chaney house, Raider jumped to the ground and began to survey the area.

Daniels thought he looked like an Indian with his nose to the ground. The sheriff got down and started to peruse the dirt, but there didn't seem to be much to look at.

"No wolf tracks here," the sheriff offered, "much less the tracks of one that walks on two legs."

Raider was stymied. "Shit. Look at that. Somebody brushed the ground with bush or a broom to cover up the tracks."

Daniels gazed at the house, which was still standing. "Thought you slung a fire in the kitchen?"

Raider's face slacked. "I did. Somebody musta put it out."

"That Indian girl who ain't around no more?"

"She left with me. Come, I'll show you what I did."

They walked through the house, making for the kitchen.

Raider felt his heart thumping again. It sure didn't look too good. In the bright rays of the sun, his story seemed stupid. Hell, he wouldn't have believed it if he hadn't lived the whole thing.

"There," he said, pointing to the burns on the wall. "I started that fire to keep the others away. Somebody musta come an' put it out."

"Who?"

Raider looked at the floor. "The same one who took away the body of that dead animal. Here, fresh blood. It's still sticky."

The sheriff still wasn't convinced. "That blood could be from the hock of the stallion. You coulda planted all this stuff to make it look like there was trouble here."

Raider was suddenly short on patience. "Why the hell would I do a stupid thing like that?"

Daniels shrugged. "Well, seems if Sharper was involved in all this, maybe he was too good at hidin' the evidence. So you shot him and then made it look like his throat was tore out by some animal."

The big man rolled his eyes. "That ain't my way, Daniels. I ain't never railroaded anyone in my whole born days. Guilty or innocent, I always get to the truth afore I point the finger."

Daniels sighed, shaking his head. "Aw right, s'pose you tell me what happened to Sharper and the Mex?"

"I been studyin' on that. Only thing I can figger is that they were workin' with somebody but the partner thought he was gettin' a raw deal. He turned on his boss, figgered to branch out on his own."

"Why?"

Raider looked away. "I ain't sure. Mebbe he just got sick o' what he did t' the Chaneys. Figgered to end it once an' for all. Or mebbe it's somethin' else. Somethin' I need t' find out."

Daniels stared at the burn marks on the wall. "Well, somebody started a fire and somebody put it out. Think it was the two-legged wolf you saw?"

Raider considered kicking his ass right there. The rage welled inside him. He never got used to the stupidity of lawmen. Or any other kind of stupidity for that matter.

"A man can't change into a wolf," the sheriff offered.

"No, but he can put on a mask. And as far as I can see, he can control a whole pack of animals. Come on out back. Let's see if we can find some other sign of what I saw."

"You sure you saw it, Pinkerton?"

"Kiss my ass, Daniels."

He stormed into the backyard.

Daniels came after him.

Raider shook his head. "Same thing. The ground has been swept. Might as well see if my stuff is still in the barn."

"You left your gear behind?"

"Hey, when they come after me, I didn't stay 'round long 'nough t' saddle up, sheriff. I was in a hurry."

His gear was there, undisturbed, in the stable.

Daniels tipped back his hat. "Well, somethin' happened here. I ain't egg-zackly sure what it was. You stirred up a fuss, Raider, but I ain't sure it was a real one. You wasn't drinkin', was you?"

He scowled at the lawman. "Where's the nearest place t' get a mount?"

"Back in town."

"We cain't both ride back on your horse, not if I drag this saddle along."

Daniels shrugged. "Leave it. You can come back to pick it up later."

Raider grabbed his saddlebags. "I'm takin' these."

"Funny,"the sheriff said, "if there was somebody else here, why didn't he take your gear?"

"Mebbe the man-wolf don't know how to ride," the big man replied. Daniels didn't think that was funny at all.

Yellow Fox had fled when she saw the glint of the sheriff's badge. She didn't like lawmen or soldiers or Indian agents. They all had one thing in common—trying to keep her people on the reservations.

That no longer mattered to Yellow Fox. She only wanted to get north again, to go back to the mission. Finding her brother didn't seem important anymore. She would stay with the fathers, maybe even find another man to marry—a man who didn't mind that she was a half-breed. *Half-breed*. The word cut her like a knife. She had heard it for the first time when she was a little girl. But that didn't seem to matter, either.

She hurried along, making for the mountains in the distance. The path to home led through the mountains. Maybe she would meet her brother along the way. He probably wouldn't even be glad to see her.

She stopped to catch her breath, peering back to the south. She was sorry to leave the kind man who had helped her. He had brought her the first pleasure that she had known since the death of her husband. But it was all over now and the only thing that lay ahead was the north.

Her feet were sore and tender but she went on. If her luck held, she'd be able to find the same path that had led her through the mountains the first time. The peaks got closer and closer. It might take her a week to get home, but she didn't care. She just wanted to be away from Texas.

The path led upward, toward the pass. As soon as she started on the trail, she began to hear them. Clicking feet, claws on rock. She'd turn to look, to catch the fleeting glimpse of a tail, the twitching of an ear. They were following her. They had come back: the creatures from the night before.

Only the cowboy wasn't here to save her. Still, she tried to run. Her lungs ached as she climbed. The trail grew steeper. Her legs were becoming weak from the constant climbing.

The creatures were getting closer.

She finally slumped in the path, crying, unable to go on.

They came out from behind the rocks, growling, stalking, glaring at her. All but one of them walked on four legs. He had a head like a wolf, and claws.

She closed her eyes, wondering how long it would take them to kill her.

CHAPTER SIXTEEN

The honest townsfolk gawked at the rough pair who rode in on the sheriff's horse. They weren't quite sure what to think of the big Pinkerton and the tales of the Wolfbrand. They just wanted to be protected in their beds while they slept tight. Raider couldn't really blame them.

Daniels reined up in front of his office.

Raider slid off the back of the chestnut.

"Where you goin'?" the sheriff asked.

"Don't worry, Bit. I'll be back."

He started off toward the livery. He wanted to tell the stable man about the stallion, before the wolves got it. If they hadn't attacked the horse already, the livery might recover some of its loss.

The livery man wasn't glad to hear that the stallion had been left at the Sharper place. Mr. Sharper might take the horse for his own. Raider said he doubted that the merchant would mind. No need to tell the man that Sharper had been killed by the Wolfbrand. He caught himself thinking it. *Wolfbrand*: the two-legged animal with the pointed snout. Damn it, that had to be a wolf mask. No man could change himself into an animal. And how the hell did he get the wolves to follow him?

The livery man asked if Raider was all right.

He nodded and turned away, saying over his shoulder that he would be back later for his own mount.

"One more thing," the man called.

Raider glanced toward the orange shimmer of the forge. "Yeah?"

"That stallion ain't mine. It belongs to Mr. Chaney. His son used to ride it all the time. I think the boy even broke it from a colt."

The big man grimaced. "Damn."

"You gonna tell him about leavin' the stallion out there?"

Raider nodded. "I reckon I should, seein's how I'm the one what left it there. Damn."

"You look spooked, mister."

His black eyes narrowed. "Don't let it worry."

"I won't. If you see Mr. Sharper, tell him he still owes me for shoein' those two draft animals."

"He might be a little late payin' you."

"I don't care, as long as I get it. He's a pretty good man, Mr. Sharper is. Never stiffed me yet."

Raider left the livery, thinking that it was better to speak kindly of the dead. He wondered how long it would take for the merchant to be missed. Would the sheriff spread the news himself? Not if he was smart. No need to get the town charged up about a wolf pack led by a man who could change into a wolf—or a wolf mask.

The Wolfbrand hadn't come to Odessa—not yet anyway.

The afternoon was still hot and dusty. Raider stood in the middle of the street, cogitating, thinking what he should do next.

Chaney had to be told about the stallion. Best to get the worst over with in a hurry.

He walked along the line of warehouses, until he saw the big sign with Jubal Chaney's name across the wall.

The older gentleman sat in his office, staring blankly ahead as Raider filled the doorway.

"You're back," he said, lifting his white-ringed eyes. "Please, sit down. We were worried about you."

Raider plopped down in the wooden chair.

"You want whiskey?" Chaney asked.

The big man nodded. "Just a snort. I got some news for you, Chaney. I had t' leave that stallion out at Sharper's place."

Chaney frowned. "Why?"

"That's the other news. I found out what killed your family."

The old merchant poured a shot of whiskey and pushed it across his desk to Raider. "Did you kill the bastard?"

He knocked back the hooch and asked for another. When his throat was burning, he said: "Well, I ain't killed nobody so far. Sharper's dead, though."

"Really?"

He nodded. "Killed by wolves, I'm pretty sure. Killed just like your kin. I'm guessin' he was double-crossed by his pardner."

Chaney had started to cry. "My God. My God."

"Yeah, well, we may need the help of providence if I'm gonna figger this thing, Chaney."

He wiped his white-ringed eyes. "I thought you said you knew who killed my family. You—"

"I saw 'em. A bunch of 'em. But I still don't know who they are."

Slowly, in as much detail as he could remember, Raider described the events of the previous day and night. Chaney sat agape, unable to take it all in. Raider had to admit to himself that the whole thing sounded pretty farfetched, but he had to say it again, to see if he could remember anything that might help him. He managed to leave out the part about the girl. No need to bring her up again. Not if she wasn't there to corroborate his story.

Chaney put his face in his hands.

"You can fire me if you want," Raider said. "I know it don't sound like it coulda happened, but it did."

Chaney shook his head. "No. You've gotten closer than that bumbling sheriff. But, well, doesn't this mean Sharper wasn't involved? I mean, he is dead after all."

The big man shrugged. "It ain't important now. I gotta find where that wolf pack is hidin'. I'm willin' t' bet that they're holed up in the mountains. There's plenty o' room t' hide up there."

Chaney gazed hopefully at the tall Pinkerton. "Then you're going to stay on the case?"

"Sure, why wouldn't I?"

Chaney lifted a piece of paper from his desk. "A telegram came in for you around noon. Here, read it."

Raider unfolded the message.

NEED YOUR HELP AT ONCE. ADVISE OF YOUR LOCATION. WAGNER.

Raider grimaced. "Damn him! I'm not through with this case."

"Your agency has other ideas for you," Chaney said sadly. "And you seem to be getting so close."

Raider crushed the piece of paper in his hand. "I never got this message. Understand, Chaney?"

"But—"

"You want me on the case?"

"You know I do."

Raider nodded. "Then I never got it. Did I?"

The old man smiled a little. "No. You didn't."

They both had a shot of whiskey.

"Wolves," Chaney said finally with a shudder.

"I seen 'em close-like," Raider offered. "They were quick. An'—well, there was this little fire out at your place."

"Did you—"

"I didn't burn it down," Raider said. "An'—well, it sounds loco, but that wolf thing musta put the fire out. I killed one o' his dogs in the kitchen. The window is kinda broke."

Chaney leaned back, exhaling. "I don't care about any of that. I just want you to avenge the death of my family. Do you hear me?"

"I'm gonna try, Chaney."

"Thank you, Raider. I'll see to it that I forward your fee to the agency at once."

The big man stood up. "Yeah, well, don't tell 'em I'm around. Say that I rode out or somethin' if you have to. But don't tell 'em you seen me. I wanna stay on this thing till I finish. Ain't one for leavin' the barn door open when it can be shut." He started for the door.

"Where are you going?" Chaney asked.

"To get a bath, some grub, and some shut-eye. This thing moves at night, so that's when I'm gonna move, too.'' Raider stared at the old gent. ''You gonna be safe here, Chaney?''

''I have been so far. Just do what I hired you to do, Raider. Don't worry about me. Worry about those wolves.''

''More than you know, Jubal. More than you know.''

Raider felt better as he strode back toward the sheriff's office. Chaney seemed pleased with the investigation. Why shouldn't he be? No one else had been able to nail down the cause of his family's demise. Raider wasn't even sure he had the right slant to finish the wolf pack.

They had been real: devil-eyed, slack-jawed. Only a rattlesnake or a bull conjured up a more sinister image of the evil face of Satan. How much longer would he see them in his dreams?

Better to stay steady, get organized. He needed shells for his rifle, which had been left in the sheriff's care. A map of the mountain area wouldn't hurt. He could get some locals to point out some good hiding spots.

When he turned onto the main thoroughfare, Raider realized that he didn't need the sheriff's hassels right away. He wanted a bath and some food. He had no taste for women now, not after Yellow Fox. She had taken care of him for a while, at least until the case was finished.

He found a clean bathhouse where a Mexican woman washed and ironed his clothes. There was even a barber in front of the bathhouse. Raider had a shave and a haircut. The barber asked him questions that the big man chose to ignore.

Looking clean and polished, he returned to the bar and ordered a steak with his beer. The bartender served the meat with potatoes and onions, just the way Raider liked it. He kept draining his mug, putting off the inevitable meeting with Daniels. How the hell was he going to get the sheriff to believe him?

''Pinkerton!''

Raider turned away from the bar to see the lawman standing behind him. ''I was just comin' t' see you, Bit. Let me buy you a drink.''

''Can't do it, Raider.''

He heard rifle levers rattling.

Daniels thumbed back the hammer of his own pistol. "You're gonna have to come with me, big man."

Raider eased around, wondering if this was some kind of joke. The sheriff had brought two men to back him up. No joke. Raider started to lower his hand to the butt of the Colt.

"Ain't too healthy to let that hand hang any farther," Daniels said. "Just turn back around and put your hands on the bar."

"Why are you doin' this, Daniels?"

"Takin' you in for the murder of John Sharper," the lawman replied. "Do like I say, big man. Turn around."

"You know I didn't kill him, sheriff!"

Daniels motioned with the barrel of his weapon. "I don't want to kill you, boy. You're smart. I gotta give you that. But you and I both know it was Sharper what hurt Chaney and his family. He killed those dogs. Then you killed him, 'cause you knew the truth all along."

"Maybe Sharper didn't—"

"Boys!"

Raider couldn't argue with the two riflemen.

He turned around and put his hands on the bar.

"You can lock me up," he told them, "but the Wolfbrand'll still be loose. You hear me, Daniels?"

"Shut up, Pinkerton."

He said it again, so the word would spread around town. Wolfbrand. All heads turned to listen as Raider wondered aloud how long it would take the Wolfbrand to hit Odessa.

Two days had passed before Wagner received the telegram from Odessa.

The telegraph operator brought it in person, but this time Wagner sent him away without a gratuity. He wanted to be alone when he read the message. Raider would probably refuse to do as he was told. The big lug never liked to quit before a case was completed. Such pride and arrogance. But then, that was what made him an effective agent.

The wire was worse than Wagner could have imagined. "Oh no, they've put him in jail again."

Allan Pinkerton had emerged from his office just in time to hear Wagner's disappointed tone. "Put who in jail?"

Wagner held out the message for his superior. "Raider. He's locked up on a murder charge."

"Him and Stokes both in jail. Blast. All right, do what you can. See if we can hire a lawyer. Contact the governor of Texas if you have to."

Wagner nodded. Why did this have to happen now? Raider in jail. In the back of his mind, Wagner entertained notions that the big galoot just might be guilty!

Things weren't right at all: Fuzzy images, out-of-focus shapes. Raider was younger and his old partner, Doc Weatherbee, had come back. They were somewhere in Montana near the high forests. It was a cool, autumn day.

"Look here, Doc," Raider heard himself saying. "Look at these pups. Ain't they somethin'?"

Doc leaned over to look at the pups. "Hmm. Precious."

Raider was puzzled. How the hell had Doc come back? Had he left his wife to return to service for Allan Pinkerton? Come all the way from back east to help Raider again?

"Doc, when did you get back?"

The sandy-haired gentleman ignored the question. He just looked at the old Indian man with a basketful of pups. How much did the man want for the little animals? Doc asked. Anything. Anything at all.

"Funny looking creatures," Doc said.

The Indian man said they were half wolf, half dog. Special animals with powers from the Great Spirit. Doc could have one for a dollar.

Raider looked at his partner. "Doc. Doc, you can help. See, I'm in trouble over in Odessa and you could—"

Raider sat up on the jailhouse cot.

"Doc?"

Sweat poured off him. It had been a dream.

He remembered the time they had met the old man with the pups. His face slacked. That was it! That was how the killer had done it. But the knowledge wouldn't help with him sitting in Bit Daniels's lockup.

The sheriff appeared at the door to the cell room. "You okay, Raider? I heard you cryin' out."

The big man scowled at his jailer. "You better let me the hell outta here, Daniels. 'Fore it's too late."

Daniels grinned smugly. "No wolves have attacked us yet, Pinkerton. Ain't seen nary a one."

"Suit yourself. Don't say I didn't warn you. You might be sayin' you're sorry t' me one o' these days."

"Two days and no trouble," the sheriff went on. "I reckon I was right about you, big man. Makes me kinda sad, though. I was sort of startin' to like you."

"Save it for your friends, sheriff. Any word from the home office?"

Daniels shook his head. "Not yet. You think they'll help?"

"Prob'ly send a lawbook thumper," Raider replied. "That way it'll all be official when you hang me."

The sheriff chortled a little. "You won't hang, Raider. Not with Sharper's dirty doin's. Might spend some time in the territorial prison, though."

Raider leaned back on the cot. "State prison," he corrected. "Texas has been a state for a long time."

"Well, you know what I mean." Daniels closed the door to the cell room.

Raider lay on the cot, looking at the sky through the barred window. It was late afternoon, soon to be dusk.

Maybe Daniels was right. Maybe it was over: no more wolves, no more killing. Raider knew better, but there wasn't a thing he could do about it in the jailhouse.

Doc tickled the stomach of one of the puppies, bickering with the old Indian man.

Suddenly, the gray-haired Apache began to change. He sprouted ears and grew fangs. He became the two-legged creature that Raider had seen in front of Chaney's ranch house.

The man-wolf attacked Doc Weatherbee.

Raider drew his Colt, but the gun kept misfiring.

Blood sprayed from Doc's neck. His throat disappeared.

The hammer clicked harmlessly.

Doc was going to die.

Click. Click.

Raider sat up again. His shirt had soaked through with perspiration. Night had fallen over the Odessa lockup. There was a shadow at the small window, a shape that made the same clicking noise as in Raider's dream.

Two eyes loomed out of the darkness: white eyes, wolf eyes.

For a moment, Raider thought the pack had come back to get him.

But the strange white eyes belonged to Jubal Chaney.

"Raider?"

The big man came off the cot, pulling himself close to the window. "Chaney, how come you waited so long t' visit me?"

"Shh. Daniels might come back. Here." Jubal Chaney passed a rope through the window. Raider knew what to do. He tied the rope around the bars and then stood back. Chaney had a horse outside. Raider watched as the bars began to give way. Iron broke from plaster. A huge hole appeared in the wall.

Raider squirmed through the opening.

Chaney handed him the reins of the gray gelding. "Here. Go on, take it. And don't come back to Odessa until you find out who killed my family."

Raider took the reins. "I'll need a gun."

"Your Colt and your rifle are on the saddle. I sent someone to find the black, so I had him pick up your saddle at my place. Said the kitchen wasn't burned too badly."

"How's the stallion?"

Chaney frowned. "Fine. Now get on your way."

Raider eyed the old gentleman. "I don't have to ask why you're doin' this. You want revenge. Your man see any wolf sign at your place?"

"None that I know of. Hurry, somebody may have heard that wall give way."

Raider swung into the saddle. "You got my guns."

"Daniels brought them to me. Said I should hang on to them until the trial. He also said he thought Sharper and those dogs had killed my family."

"We both know better."

"Just go, Raider."

A yell resounded from the jailhouse. "What the hell!"

"It's Daniels," Chaney cried.

Raider spurred the gelding into the alley.

He'd just have to let Chaney take his chances with the lawman.

Shots erupted as Daniels fired through the hole in the wall.

But Raider was long gone, heading northwest.

The gray was strong, ready to fly. A hot wind blew from behind, pushing him into the dark.

He had to find an old Apache named Walking Eagle. Maybe the medicine man could tell him about the Wolfbrand.

At least he could avoid the mountains on his route to the reservation. He didn't want to fight the wolves again until he knew exactly how to stop them.

"Raider has escaped from jail!" Wagner cried.

Pinkerton burst out of his office. "What?"

"Someone sprung him by pulling out the bars in the window of his cell. This sheriff—Daniels, I believe—says that he holds us responsible for the damages. Raider is now a wanted man."

The clerks began to whisper among themselves. Raider was something of a legend in the minds of the office-bound employees. Wagner silenced them with a harsh glance.

Pinkerton had turned bright red. "That does it. He's fired! On his own. I won't stand for this."

He slammed the door to his office, retreating into his private sanctuary.

Wagner nodded to one of his assistants. He wasn't giving up on Raider; not yet. He'd have to find someone to look into the matter. Maybe a team of men. He just hoped that he wasn't too late.

No one could take Raider, he thought, not unless they were awfully lucky, not unless the big man's luck finally ran out on him.

Raider pressed on in the hunt, riding west into New Mexico. He had run the gray to the brink. Two days in the saddle, mostly at night. Catnaps before daybreak, riding into the next morning. He prayed that the animal wouldn't die under him.

He found water twice. Then it rained.

How long would it take him to get into Apache country?

The third day he rested for several hours, letting the gray drink by a brook that was swollen from summer rains.

He must be close to the reservation, unless he had come too far north.

If he cut back south, he might run into a posse. His better sense told him that Bit Daniels was the kind of lawman who would have turned back at the New Mexico border. Daniels wasn't crazy enough to come into Apache country. Still, a local lawman could show surprising courage sometimes, so there was no sense in being careless.

On the fifth day, he did swing south, making sure to keep an eye on the horizon. A posse stirred up a lot of dust. Apaches, on the other hand, could come on you pretty quick, without any warning.

As the ground began to rise into short ridges and low mesas, Raider caught the horse-sign in the sand: manure, probably from unshod Indian ponies. He had crossed into Apache country.

It didn't take long for him to find them. It was really the other way around. Five young braves riding bareback, two of them carrying rifles, began to follow him on a ridge, keeping their distance until they were in sight of the tribal encampment.

Raider looked down into the valley, gazing toward the reservation.

The braves fell in beside him.

Raider tipped his hat. "Lookin' for Walkin' Eagle."

There was no reply from the stoic warriors. They just surrounded him, took his guns, and then led him into camp.

CHAPTER SEVENTEEN

The Apache braves delivered Raider to the largest teepee in the circle of the village. Their chief lived in the big tent. Raider just hoped that Walking Eagle would talk to him.

One of them motioned for him to dismount.

Raider swung slowly out of the saddle.

They probably wouldn't kill him unless he tried to hurt someone. They might fool with him a little. Like playing with a mouse in a bucket, they might torment him before they let him go.

"I gotta talk to Walkin' Eagle," he said again.

Two of them stepped up behind him, tying his hands with rawhide thongs. He stayed still. It made sense that they would want to keep their chief safe from the intruder.

What if they decided to go back to the old days and string him up just for a few laughs?

They urged him into the big teepee. When his eyes adjusted to the dim light, he saw three old men sitting in front of a smouldering fire. They looked at him, not showing much sign of emotion. Lined faces, weathered skin, a rheumy look in their eyes. Raider kept his mouth shut, waiting for them to address him.

The old man in the middle spoke first. "You have come onto our land."

Raider nodded. "Yes, sir."

"Why have you done this? The bluecoats say this land is ours. And you come here on your own."

"I ain't no bluecoat," Raider replied. "I'm a Pinkerton agent. Name's Raider. I'm lookin' for Walkin' Eagle. Gotta talk t' him about the Wolfbrand."

The old man looked to both sides of him. The other men got up and left. Then the old Apache clapped his hands and one of the younger men came in to cut Raider's rawhide bonds.

"Thanks," he said to the chief. "I'm takin' you t' be Walkin' Eagle."

"Sit there and tell me why the eagle would walk."

Raider took his place on the other side of the fire, sitting cross-legged like the old man. "I reckon a eagle would walk if he couldn't fly."

"I am Walking Eagle."

Raider stared into the old man's eyes. He considered asking about the girl, Yellow Fox, but he didn't want to change course. He had come to ask about something else.

"Chief, do you know about the Wolfbrand?"

Walking Eagle meshed his fingers together. "The spirits of man and wolf come together. The bodies come together. Great medicine."

The big man decided to take a chance. "Some say that you conjured the Wolfbrand, chief. They say it's your magic."

Walking Eagle smirked at him. "I have no magic. The Wolfbrand is the spirit of our people."

"Does your spirit still wanna kill the white man? To tear out his throat? To kill innocent boys an' women?"

The smirk disappeared. "Those things have not happened."

Raider nodded. "They have. To a man named Chaney. A man like you who minds his own business."

"I have not heard of this."

Raider made a sweeping gesture. "No, 'cause you been here

in New Mexico. These goin's on are down in Texas. There's a man leadin' a pack o' wolves, chief. I seen him. An' I killed a couple of 'em so I'm bettin' he ain't gonna be my friend. An' I sure as hell ain't gonna be his."

Walking Eagle stared into the fire. "Killing has made me sick, Pinkerton. I am sad to hear about this."

"Then help me, chief. With magic or just with words."

They were silent for a long time. Raider could see the old man thinking it over. Walking Eagle had probably never believed in the Wolfbrand. But now it had cropped up to haunt him.

"I will not use my magic," Walking Eagle said finally. "But you can hear the name of Black Dog."

Raider frowned at the old boy. "Black Dog? I thought he was killed by the soldiers when he was runnin' with those other renegades."

Walking Eagle shook his head. "Black Dog. If you find him, then you will find the Wolfbrand."

"Black Dog. Damn."

The old chief pointed toward the entrance of the tent. He wanted Raider to leave, but the big man pressed him again.

"Walkin' Eagle, do you know Yellow Fox? She's—"

Walking Eagle clapped his hands. "Go."

Two of the braves reappeared to escort Raider back to his horse.

Black Dog. That was something. Maybe he could find some trace of the renegade along the border. At least he had a name to go on. And the Apaches hadn't killed him. They even gave him back his guns. He spurred the gray, driving away from the village.

Maybe things had finally started to fall into place. Raider headed back to Texas to see if he could catch a wolf.

Black Dog. Everybody Raider met on the way seemed to know the name. Black Dog had stolen a pig in Magala. Some white woman claimed that Black Dog had been peeking into her window at night in Carlsbad. Two down-on-their-luck prospectors claimed that Black Dog had robbed them of their last dollar not a week ago.

Black Dog: a character along the New Mexico/Texas border. He never seemed to hurt anyone. He just stole and acted loco.

Some said he lived in the mountains. Others claimed he slept on the plain, like a heathen savage.

Black Dog had made something of a name for himself, although Raider couldn't figure out why he hadn't heard of the renegade's resurrection.

Maybe somebody else was using the renegade's name or maybe he really was alive and had learned how to train a pack of wolves to do his bidding.

He sure as hell couldn't change himself into a wolf. Could he?

Raider held a steady course to the south, until he could see the mountains in the distance.

Black Dog was supposed to be hiding somewhere in the blind ridges and hollows of the Guadalupes.

Raider had lost the trail of the Wolfbrand in the same region.

It struck him that he had wasted too much time going north. Of course the man-wolf was in the mountains. He hadn't needed Walking Eagle to tell him that. Still, the old chief had turned the monster into a man, somebody who had weaknesses like any other man.

He reined up and gazed toward the mountains. Heat lines shimmered on the plain. He wondered where the wolf pack was hiding.

What if he just rode into the mountains and faced them? That would be stupid, he decided. Why press them on their own turf? He would make them come to him.

The mountains seemed so peaceful.

Why the hell had Black Dog come after Chaney?

He thought about the girl. Walking Eagle hadn't even wanted to hear her name. Apaches could be real mean to one another. Walking Eagle obviously hated Black Dog or he wouldn't have given his name to Raider in the first place.

He shook off the chill in his shoulders.

The mountain passes were too narrow. And it would be dark soon. No need to take a chance with a night passage through the peaks.

He'd take the long way around. It meant more time, but he wasn't ready to face the wolf. Not yet.

He had to speak to Jubal Chaney first.

And that meant sneaking back into Odessa, where Raider was still a wanted man.

William Wagner glanced up from his desk as the telegraph operator came through the door. The man was smiling. He probably had news of Raider or Stokes, both of whom were still in trouble.

"Well?" Wagner asked.

"Stokes is out on bail," the man replied.

Wagner sighed. "Finally. Anything about Raider?"

"No, sir. Not since that last one."

"Two weeks," Wagner said. "I haven't heard a word from him."

Allan Pinkerton burst in through the front door. He grimaced when he saw the telegraph man. Pinkerton hated getting bad news and he sometimes tended to blame the messenger.

Wagner ushered the smiling fool toward the exit. "Thank you."

"What? What is it?" Pinkerton insisted.

"Stokes is out of jail," Wagner replied.

The telegraph man couldn't help but get into the act. "No word from Raider, though."

Pinkerton erupted. "That Arkansas ridgerunner no longer works for this agency. Do you hear me? I fired him."

Wagner pushed the clerk through the door, glaring at him. "See what you've done!"

"Wanted criminals do not work for this agency!" Pinkerton railed.

He stormed off into his office.

Wagner closed the front door and leaned back against it.

He didn't have the manpower to send someone after Raider, not right away. For the time being, Raider would stay a wanted man. The rough-hewn cowboy from Arkansas was on his own.

A hot wind blew over Odessa.

Raider had waited until nightfall to enter the town. He had come in on foot, through the widow's property. That trail left him in front of the warehouses on the edge of town. The street was quiet. Dust stirred in front of Jubal Chaney's place.

Raider studied it for a while but there were no signs of movement inside the warehouse. What if the pack had come for Chaney?

Somehow Raider felt the merchant was still alive. Maybe the Wolfbrand wanted him that way. What kind of injustice would allow a man to torture another man by killing off his family in such a heinous way? Sometimes men didn't need reasons for their wickedness.

There were enough shadows to hide his approach. He eased to the warehouse door, testing to see if it was open. It was unlocked. A lamp burned inside Chaney's office. At least the merchant was alive.

Raider stepped into the warehouse, closing the door behind him.

"That's far enough." The voice had come from the other side of the building. Someone moved in the shadows.

Raider stayed still, his hand hovering over the butt of the Colt. "It's me, Mr. Chaney. I come back." He had recognized the old man's voice.

Chaney stepped forward, holding a shotgun on him. "Raider?"

"Yes, sir."

He stared down the barrel of the scattergun.

"Raider!"

"Wanna lower that barrel, Mr. Chaney?"

"Of course, of course."

He moved past Raider, toward the door. "I hope nobody saw you ride in. Daniels has put a price on your head."

"That fool. Nobody saw me. I walked in."

Chaney gestured toward his office. "Here, let's have whiskey. I need a drink." The old merchant looked pale and worn.

"You feelin' aw right, Mr. Chaney?"

He sighed. "I'm tired, Raider. Just tired."

Raider sat down in one of the wooden chairs.

Chaney waddled behind his desk and produced the bottle. "Did you find anything?" he asked, pushing the shot toward Raider.

The whiskey burned, but it took the edge off. "Well, Walkin' Eagle put me in the direction of a man named Black Dog."

"I thought he was dead," Chaney rejoined.

"That ain't the word goin' 'round."

Chaney grimaced. "What about Black Dog?"

"I don't know. He might be the one b'hind this wolf business. Walkin' Eagle seemed t' think so. I wasted my time, except to let things cool off around Odessa."

"Daniels has begun to run for reelection on the claim that he's going to bring you in for the death of Sharper."

Raider laughed.

"You find that funny?"

The big man smiled at his employer. "Wouldn't he have a fit if I walked down Main Street and called him out. Gunfight, right there in the street. Hell, the sheriff'd prob'ly have t' go t' the saloon for a drink. His hand would be shakin' like a willow leaf."

Chaney poured two more shots.

Raider eyed the old gent. "Chaney, you gotta tell me somethin'."

"If I can help—"

"Why the hell would somebody wanna kill your family? Tell me that. Can you think of a single reason?"

Chaney started to cry again. "No. None. I've tried to remember my life, to recall what I had done to deserve this, but I can't. Even though I was somewhat of a rounder as a young man, I still don't know what sin I've been paying for."

"Well, this Black Dog came after you. He went to a lotta trouble t' make it look like he could change into a wolf. And there don't seem t' be no reason for it."

Chaney held out his hands. "I've never met Black Dog. The only Apache I've ever seen was a scrubwoman who worked for my family. But she was a nice woman. She chose to go north, back to the reservation. And that's been twenty odd years ago."

"Afore the war," Raider offered.

Chaney nodded. "There was trouble with the Apache back then, but we stood up to them. I never fought in the wars, but my brothers did. Why, my second cousins once removed were there at the Alamo."

Raider waved him off. "Don't worry 'bout that stuff now, Chaney. We gotta see what's really here. We gotta find a way t' stop those wolves an' I think I might know how t' do it."

Chaney eyed him cautiously. "Raider, you're a wanted man. You can't stay in Odessa."

"No, I cain't stay here. I don't wanna stay here neither. If I'm gonna stop this Wolfbrand, I gotta meet him halfway or he won't come t' me."

The old man leaned forward. "I'm with you, Raider. Whatever

I can do. If it means catching the thing that killed my family—"

"You're gonna have t' come with me, Chaney. It might mean riskin' your life. You up to it?"

"Life? I have no life. Only the lonely days of remembering my family as they were when they were alive. Yes, I'll risk my life. That doesn't seem like much of a gamble these days."

Raider exhaled. "Chaney, I seen these things. You're gonna need that scattergun. They're quick an' they're mean."

"Didn't you kill two of them?"

"One that I know of," the big man replied. "I mighta got another one."

Chaney shook his head in disbelief. "How? How could a man teach a pack of wolves to kill for him?"

"I think I figgered that one out already," Raider said. He told Chaney his theory.

The old gent nodded appreciatively. "I'd never have thought of that."

"Came to me in a dream," Raider replied.

Chaney shuddered. "Dreams. I've come to hate them lately. I hope I never dream again."

Raider figured that facing the wolf demon would be more like a nightmare, but they had to lay the snare and they had to do it at Chaney's country home.

If the Wolfbrand wanted the old man—dead or alive—it would come after him at the ranch.

Raider just hoped he could be ready when it happened.

Preparations for the wolf trap took a while because the old man had to do everything himself. Raider couldn't operate in the daytime because he would be recognized immediately. The big man hated hiding while Chaney worked, but what else could he do?

Finally, after a couple of days, Chaney drove the loaded buckboard out of the warehouse, locking the door behind him.

Raider followed in the shadows, staying close enough to see him. When the sun went down, he joined Chaney and rode alongside him. It took them a day and a night to get to Chaney's ranch. Raider had to stay out of sight when they finally got there, at least during daylight.

Chaney was the one that had to be seen. It might take a while to draw out the wolf pack, but sooner or later word would get around that the old man was living alone at his ranch. If they wanted Chaney, they would come for him.

Raider had to wonder why they hadn't already made an attempt on the old man. It seemed as if they wanted him alive. The whole thing still didn't make any sense. Maybe it would straighten out as they went along.

He watched from the window as Chaney walked around the property.

"That's right, Jubal. Let 'em see you. It's broad daylight."

Chaney seemed to enjoy the game. He even looked better. Then again, he hadn't seen the wolves himself. Maybe it was better if he didn't know what to expect. Raider would be there with his guns and his traps.

The big man remembered the way the pack had moved: too damned fast.

And the one on two legs kept coming at him from out of the dark. Those damned wolf dreams. He wished like hell they would go away.

The next night, Raider went to work under the cover of darkness. He set his traps and rigged his snares. When he was ready, he climbed onto the roof where he also had a heavy net. Chaney had gotten him everything he had asked for.

The old man came up to join him. It took a while for Chaney to ascend the ladder, but he sat down next to Raider, offering him a pull from a whiskey bottle. The old guy loved his hooch.

Raider declined the drink. "Where's your scattergun?"

"Downstairs," Chaney replied.

They both peered into the darkness.

"Do you really think they'll come?" Chaney asked.

Raider tipped back his Stetson. "They killed your family, so they must want somethin' from you."

"I wish they'd come and get it over with."

Raider gestured to the east. "Mebbe tonight."

Chaney shuddered when he gazed toward the horizon. "Is it that time already? My God."

Raider figured it was just what they needed. A full moon rose bright and new in the east. They sat on the roof, listening for the howl of the wolf pack as the light grew higher in the sky.

Raider stiffened when he saw the figure moving toward the house. It came slowly and steadily, making its way in the shadows. He picked it up when it came within a couple of hundred yards of the house, moving on two legs. He didn't see the wolf pack behind the figure, but it couldn't be too far away.

He nudged Chaney, who had fallen asleep.

"What—"

"Shh."

Raider pointed to the north. "Comin' this way."

"I don't see it." Chaney squinted. "No, I don't."

"Then stay here."

Raider stood, keeping his balance on the slant of the roof.

Chaney grabbed his leg. "Are you going to leave me alone?"

Raider tossed him the Colt. "Here. I'm keepin' the rifle for myself. Just stay here till I tell you different. If anythin' comes at you real quick like, then shoot it."

"But—"

"I gotta do this, Chaney. And you gotta help. Now shut up before we scare it off."

It. Chaney hated the sound of the word. He clutched Raider's Colt to his chest, waiting for the worst.

Raider stepped down to the edge of the roof. He hunkered there, watching the shadows. The thing was still coming—faster now. He listened for the panting of dogs but didn't hear a thing. It moved like an Indian: silent,steady. It stopped a hundred feet in front of the house, watching the place.

Chaney had lighted a single lamp inside. No need to have too many lights to scare it away. Just let it think the old man was by himself, an easy target.

What did the man-wolf want with Chaney?

The shape started moving again, edging closer.

Raider gripped the net that lay next to him on the roof.

It had to be a man in a wolf mask. No man could change into an animal. Why the hell had Black Dog chosen Chaney? If it was Black Dog. Walking Eagle might have been lying. What if the old medicine man had really given Black Dog the power to change into a wolf?

Raider saw the outline of the form as it came under him. The moon had brought it forth. He gripped the net.

It stopped at the corner of the house, as if it were listening.

Where was the rest of the pack? Probably not too far behind.

It moved around the side of the house, coming straight beneath him.

Raider twirled the net, letting it drop. The net found its mark.

Raider dropped to the ground next to it.

The captive grunted inside the mesh. It fought to get away. Raider swung a fist and caught it squarely on the chin. It dropped like a sack of rocks. Raider lifted his rifle, waiting for the attack from the rest of the wolf pack. But it never came from the darkness.

"Chaney! Come here an' cover me!"

The old merchant peered over the edge of the roof. "What is it?"

Raider began to unfold the net. "I ain't sure. Didn't put up much of a fight, though."

When the figure rolled out of the mesh, Raider groaned. "Oh no, not her!"

"It's a girl!" Chaney cried. "An Indian girl."

"Yellow Fox," Raider moaned. "What the hell is she doin' here?"

He lifted her in his arms. The punch had knocked her cold. As he carried her toward the house, he prayed that he hadn't killed her.

CHAPTER EIGHTEEN

Raider lowered the body of Yellow Fox onto a couch in the main parlor of the ranch house.

Chaney, who had finally made it down the ladder, lighted another lamp and held it over the pretty face. "Is she still alive?"

"She's breathin'," Raider replied. "I don't know for how long, but she's still breathin'."

"Where the devil did you meet her?" the merchant asked.

Raider exhaled defeatedly. "She just sorta turned up a while back. She was with me the first time those wolves set on me."

Chaney held the light a little closer. "Hmm. A lovely little thing. I wonder why she came here?"

"Prob'ly just t' make me miserable. Stay with her Chaney. I'll get some water."

He hurried into the kitchen, returning with a bowl of water and a cloth.

Chaney studied the girl's breathing. "She may just be sleeping."

Raider nodded. "I just hope she can wake up. Damn it, why did she have t' come now?"

Raider dabbed her face with the cold cloth.

Yellow Fox stirred, but she didn't open her eyes.

Chaney rubbed his chin, still holding the lamp. "However did this delicate creature survive in the wilds of Texas?"

"She ain't that delicate. And she's been up in New Mexico, livin' at one o' them missions."

The old man frowned. "Hmm. Why wasn't she living on the reservation with her people?"

Raider touched the cloth to her lips. "I don't know, somethin' 'bout her paw bein' a white man. Here, you got somethin' t' put under her head?"

Chaney produced a round little pillow that had his family name embroidered in red stitches. "My wife made this."

Raider put the pillow under Yellow Fox's head. "Damn, look at that. Caught her square on the chin. She may not wake up for a while."

"Maybe we should try giving her whiskey," the old man suggested. "I know I could use a shot myself."

Raider agreed that the whiskey might bring her around. He didn't want any for himself though. The moon-washed night had him spooked. Best to keep his head clear for now.

"Brandy," Chaney said. "That might do it."

"Worth a try. I'd sure as hell like t' know why she came back here. I thought she'd head for home after those dogs got on us."

Chaney retrieved a soup spoon from the kitchen. He poured it full of brandy and lowered it to the girl's lips. Yellow Fox coughed but she didn't open her eyes, at least not right away.

Raider shook his head. "I killed her. I just know it. I shouldn'ta hit her so hard."

"Nonsense," Chaney replied as he poured himself some brandy, "you thought you had caught the Wolfbrand. You had no way of telling that the girl had been caught in the net."

"I reckon."

The big man felt antsy. What if the girl was some sort of setup? A distraction. At least he hadn't shot her.

"I better get back t' the roof," he told Chaney. "You stay with her. An' put that other light out. One lamp is enough. We don't want it t' think you're havin' a party."

"*It*," Chaney rejoined.

"What else you want me t' call it?"

The old man shivered. "I'm sorry."

Raider waved him off. "Aw, don't fret. At least the trap worked—on Yellow Fox—but it did work."

"How—"

"Go on," Raider urged, "say it."

"How many of them do you think there are?"

Raider calculated for a moment. "Well, I shot at least one of 'em. I found sign for ten, mebbe twelve. Hell, I reckon there's close to a dozen, give or take one or two."

Chaney moved across the room and picked up his scattergun.

"Now you're gettin' the idea, Jubal."

He handed Raider the Colt. The big man holstered up. It was time to get back to his trap; to watch over the place.

"Don't touch her, Chaney."

The old boy stiffened indignantly. "What kind of man do you think I am, anyway?"

An unlucky man, Raider thought, but he didn't say it. "Sorry, Chaney. Force o' habit. I run into a lotta stinkers in my business. Some men might take advantage of a girl like that."

"Allow me some social graces," the old merchant replied. "I'm old enough to be her father!"

Raider started for the door, picking up his rifle as he went. "Just stay low an' don't move 'round too much. If I call you, get your scattergun an' come runnin'."

Chaney said that the big man could count on him.

Raider eased out into the night. The moon was high, almost directly overhead. Maybe the creature wouldn't come tonight.

He started up the ladder, stopping halfway when he heard the woman scream. It was Yellow Fox. Apparently she had awakened and she was crying like Satan had come after her in a nightmare.

The moon stirred the pack to life. They came out of the cave, rubbing against one another. They were waiting, as was their habit, for the two-legged one. They had no idea that he had gone scouting. His absence only invoked their training, which was to stay close to the lair when the two-legged one was not there. The big male turned his nose to the breeze. He smelled the two-legged one. The others caught the scent as well.

The two-legged one approached from the east, where he had been watching the ranch house.

They tried to rub against his muzzle, the fur of their own mother.

His hands brushed them aside, causing them to fall together in one giant lump of fur. The two-legged one was angry. They sensed it.

When the two-legged one went into the cave, the big male moved in front of the pack, reestablishing his dominance.

Their master emerged from the cave. He had become angrier.

The big male watched him as he ranted in the language that they had heard from other two-legged creatures. Only the others had not smelled like their mother.

The girl was gone. She had slipped away when the two-legged one left them.

He glared at his children, his eyes burning through the layer of fur, but he could not blame them.

The girl had used a piece of broken pottery to cut her bonds. What had she been thinking? Didn't she know that he had done it all for her? Surely she would not run to the tall man.

He opened his arms to the pack. The creatures swirled around him like red leaves in a current of air.

He still had the scent of the tall man. Take them to feed. Let them open his throat.

He pointed them east and started to move. The big male led them. Their feet made little noise in the dirt. A slow, silent approach. Kill the big man, but not the old merchant. He would live. It was the tall Pinkerton that scared the Wolfbrand a little.

They held steady on the plain, making for the ranch house that shone brightly in the light of the full moon.

Yellow Fox screeched at the top of her lungs.

Raider burst into the house with his Winchester in front of him.

The girl was fighting with Chaney, who seemed to be trying to hold her down. "Help me," he called to Raider.

"What the devil happened?"

"She woke up screaming," the old man replied. "Here, you take her. She's too strong for me."

Chaney backed away from the thrashing Apache woman.

Raider slid down next to her. "Honey, I—"

She recognized him immediately. "Madre Dios, you must leave. You cannot stay here."

Raider tipped back his Stetson. "Hey, where you been, girl? I figgered you'd be halfway back to the mission by now."

Yellow Fox wrapped her arms around him and buried her face in his chest, sobbing like she had lost her last friend.

Chaney frowned disapprovingly. "I suppose your acquaintance is more intimate than I—"

Raider eyed him with a stern glance. "Let it drop, Chaney. Don't pay t' be too righteous."

The old man turned away.

Raider waited a while before he gently pushed the girl away from him. "Yellow Fox, where'd you go?"

"Into the mountains!"

Her eyes opened wide. She seemed to get more hysterical. Raider wondered what had spooked her so badly.

"Settle down, Yellow Fox."

Chaney gaped at her. "She's in a frenzy."

"The mountains!" Yellow Fox cried. "I saw them there. I saw them. They are horrible. Evil spirits. Satan himself."

Raider held her arms, staring into her white-flecked eyes. "Slower, honey. Tell me what you saw."

Chaney moved toward them. "Maybe a shot of brandy will help."

He gave it to her right from the bottle.

Yellow Fox coughed vigorously.

Raider held her close to him. The poor little thing. But she knew something and he had to get it out of her.

"Yellow Fox, if you—"

"The pack!" she cried, pushing away from him. "Wolves. I saw them. I sat with them."

Raider wondered if she had gone loco. "Where, Yellow Fox? Where did you see the pack?"

The whiskey seemed to hit bottom. Her eyes rolled. "The mountains," she slurred. "I saw them—"

"Where? Can you take me there? Yellow Fox, can you—"

"Black Dog!" she cried. "He's—"

"I know all about it, " the big man rejoined. "But honey, can you take me to their hideout?"

Her lips moved but nothing came out. She reclined on the couch, pulling her legs into her stomach.

Raider patted her shoulder. "Go to sleep, honey. I'll be here t' protect you."

Yellow Fox hugged her own knees, sobbing until her pretty eyes were shut, escaping into fitful slumber.

"Just seemed to give out," Chaney offered.

"Yeah," Raider replied, "let's hope we ain't next."

CHAPTER NINETEEN

Chaney reached for the brandy bottle. "She said she was with them. In their lair."

Raider shrugged. "Mighta been, but I doubt it. She was probably dreamin' 'bout 'em. It was all too much for her after she run off. Hell, it was a good load for me t' handle, much less that sweet little thing." He picked up his rifle.

"Raider!"

He eyed the merchant. "Yeah?"

"What if she was with them? What if she hasn't been dreaming?"

"Look at her," the big man replied. "Ain't no wolf done anythin' t' her. Hell, that bunch woulda took her apart the first chance they got."

Chaney slumped into a chair. "I suppose you're right. That look in her eyes. It reminded me of my son when they found him. His eyes were open and he—"

His voice trailed off.

Raider thought he looked pale. "You gonna make it, Chaney?"

"I don't—"

Raider suddenly raised his hand.

"What—"

"Listen, Chaney."

They both heard the second howl.

High and sinister, the wolf's cry echoed through the night.

Raider hefted his rifle. "Son of a bitch."

He told Chaney to grab the scattergun, to get ready.

The pack had returned for one more battle.

The big male turned his voice to the moon.

Suddenly the two-legged one slapped him, knocking him to the ground.

The big male fell in with the others, curling his lips a little, snarling at the leader.

There would be no more howling tonight. The approach to the house had to be silent.

Turning his eyes east, the two-legged one peered toward the oil lamps that burned in the window.

Their quarry was there, hiding inside. He would have to make sure that the old man stayed alive. The two-legged one held out his hand to the big male. His child was happy to retake the lead. They moved toward the dim ranch house, eyes straight ahead, mouths agape. They were going to hunt again, and this time, the big man would not escape.

Raider eased next to the window, peering out toward the front yard.

"See anything?" Chaney asked.

"Hush up."

His heart had picked up the beat a little. Sweat formed on his forehead and dripped down his neck. He remembered what he could of the first attack by the pack of animals. The damned thing had come straight through the window. Raider hadn't even seen him until the last second.

Chaney held his scattergun ready. "Raider—"

"Put a cork in it, Chaney. Damn."

The moon created too many shadows. A night bird flittered from the ground, its wings flashing in the glow of the full moon. Was there something moving in from the west? From the mountains?

He looked back toward the girl. Had she really been with the wolves? What if—he caught a glimpse of something moving in the corner of his eye.

Chaney saw him stiffen. "What is it?"

Raider broke for the back door. "Stay here. An' shoot the hell outta anything with fur on it."

Chaney trembled inside his suit. "But—"

"No time to jaw, Chaney."

"Should I put out the lamps?"

Raider was almost into the kitchen. "It don't matter," he called back, "they can see in the dark."

The big man left the merchant with Yellow Fox.

Chaney might have to use the scattergun before it was all over.

He slipped out the back door.

What if the pack circled around?

It wouldn't matter which direction they took if Raider was on the roof.

Some of the horses snorted from the stable. The big man tensed lifting the rifle, waiting for the shapes to come on him. Nothing rushed from the darkness. The horses continued to startle.

Raider decided not to go to the stable. The horses might smell the approaching menace—if there was something on the way.

What if the howling had been a coyote? No, he knew the difference between a coyote and a wolf.

The best vantage point was on the roof of the house. He could see in all directions from the crest of the roof. Then it wouldn't matter where the bastards came from.

The pack rested on their bellies, watching the house.

Their leader saw the big man come out. He made a hand gesture toward the pack. Two of his children rose. They were the runts of the litter. Now the time was at hand. The runts had to prove themselves. The Wolfbrand gestured again and the animals began to run toward the man behind the ranch house.

• • •

Raider was halfway up the ladder when he realized he had left his net on the ground below. He started to climb down. His back was turned as the two wolves came hell-bent with the first attack. He heard them, but by that time it was too late. One of them had jumped, grabbing the big man's leg in the meat of the calf. Raider screamed. He drew his Colt and fired back at the animal, hitting it in the head. The wolf did not let go. Raider shot it two more times before it fell away.

Blood poured down his leg, but he knew he had to climb again.

The damn pain held him still. He could barely move the leg. He was lifting it when the second animal rushed underneath him. It wanted to grab his belly, to tear into the soft part of the flesh, to rend his guts from the cavity of his torso.

Raider gaped as the open jaws flew up toward him. He lifted his body off the ladder.

The animal's teeth caught the wooden rung. It hung there for a second.

Raider tried to shoot it but the shifting weight had made the ladder give way. It fell from the eave of the roof. Raider crashed to the ground, landing on top of the wriggling canine form.

Raider saw the hateful face right there in front of him. The wolf's head showed white teeth and evil eyes. He had to shoot it.

His gun hand was trapped beneath him.

The animal struggled to get free.

Raider pulled up the Colt.

There was a cry from the wolf.

Raider stuck the bore of the pistol against the animal's head and then tripped the trigger. That was one wolf that would never bite anyone again.

He rolled off the ladder and started to crawl desperately toward the house. Stay low. What if he couldn't walk again? He hoped like hell the wolf didn't have rabies. Where were the rest of them?

The back door opened. Chaney peered out, holding his scattergun.

Raider called to him. "I'm sure glad you're a fool, Chaney."

It took a moment for the merchant to spot him on the ground. "Good God, man! What happened?"

Raider tried to raise his body. "Just get me into the house. We gotta board up the windows."

Chaney helped him into the kitchen.

Raider limped to a chair and rolled up the leg of his jeans. He took a deep breath before he looked down at the wound. Blood oozed from the fang marks, but it wasn't as bad as it could have been.

Chaney grimaced. "Lord!"

"Get me some whiskey and a bandage."

The old gent was quick to come up with both.

Raider took a stiff drink and then poured the hooch on his wounds. He grimaced with the sting. He took another drink as Chaney wrapped the bandage tightly around his bleeding calf. When the dressing had been tied off, Raider stood up again. The leg hurt but he could still walk. Some of the good feeling started to come back.

"What now?" Chaney asked.

Raider limped toward the front room. "They're gonna come after us again. And they ain't gonna like me killin' them two. I figger there's 'bout eight of 'em left, plus the Wolfbrand." He had finally started to believe in the creature.

Chaney tried to say something, but he caught the expression on Raider's rugged face. The big man looked angry. His black eyes had narrowed and he closed his mouth tightly. Raider knew the threat was serious.

It was then that Chaney experienced the darkest fear he had ever known.

The pack flinched when they heard the gunfire. They heard the yelping of their brothers. Their first instinct was to flee, but the two-legged one forced them to stay. Several of them whined until their master lowered his fist.

Two more of his children had died. The killings had to be avenged. He turned to the big male, patting his head. The animal nuzzled his hand.

They would all move together. The big male would lead the ones on four legs. The Wolfbrand urged the creature toward the house. His other children fell in, following the hunt.

The Wolfbrand circled in the opposite direction. He wanted the blood of the big man on his own maw. The moon urged him on. He lifted his pointed snout, howling as loud as he could. There was no fear left in him—just the thirst for the blood of the tall man.

CHAPTER TWENTY

Raider picked up the shotgun and handed it to Chaney. "Is there some place you can hide with the girl?"

"Up in the attic."

"Good, if you—"

Movement behind them.

Raider spun with the Colt.

Yellow Fox gaped at the barrel of the revolver. The shooting had awakened her. Tears rolled down her face.

Raider lowered the gun. "Honey, you gotta hide. The wolves have come back. Hurry. Chaney's gonna show you where t' go."

As they were turning, something began to scratch at the back door.

Raider wheeled and fanned the hammer of the Colt, sending two shots through the door.

An animal's yelping retreated into the night.

He turned back toward the main parlor. "Get a move on!"

Chaney and the girl ran ahead of him.

Raider almost had to drag the bad leg, but he could still walk. And as long as there was life left in his body, he planned to fight them.

Chaney reached for a hanging cord, pulling down the ladder that led up to the attic. "You coming with us, Raider?"

"No. I'm goin' after it."

Yellow Fox ran to the big man, throwing her arms around his waist. "You cannot kill them all."

He pushed her away. "You go with Chaney."

She looked up into his eyes. "Please. I must tell you. The Wolfbrand. It's Black Dog."

"I know—"

"Black Dog is my brother!"

Both of them gaped at her.

Raider pushed her toward Chaney. He was about to say something when the wolf crashed through the window.

The rushing weight of the animal knocked Raider to the floor. Teeth bared within inches of his face.

Raider had managed to get a hold on the animal's fur with both hands. He wrestled it, keeping the fangs away. When he rolled to his right, he forced the animal against the wall. He wanted to reach for his Colt but he couldn't let go of the fur. The teeth seemed closer. The knife in his boot wouldn't do any good. He couldn't reach it, either. He would have to try to grab for the animal's throat. His right hand gave way, freeing the creature's head. He expected to feel the teeth on his throat but the wolf's head disappeared, instead.

The explosion had come from Chaney's scattergun. He had leaned over, placing both barrels against the wolf's head. Two loads of buckshot had sent the hateful demon to perdition.

Raider jumped to his feet.

Chaney backed away, gaping at the carnage.

"Get her into the attic!" Raider cried.

Yellow Fox began to protest. "You can't kill him. Please."

But Raider was already climbing out the window. He hit the ground and hunkered low in the shadows.

There had to be a least five of them left, maybe six. Something made a snapping noise in the dark. Another yelp from a wounded animal. It cried like it was dying. One of Raider's traps had been sprung. He had stopped another one.

The big man from Arkansas peered toward the barn. His mind began to burn. He saw flames. If he could lead them there, it might work.

One last try. If he didn't get them quickly, they might turn the tables on him. His bum leg would surely slow him up. He started to move, running as fast as he could. The horses would have to be freed. No need to hurt them, too. How the hell would he set it off?

He hadn't run ten yards before he heard the howling behind him.

The pack ran to the sounds of their yelping brother. He had been caught in the jaws of the trap. They watched him die in agony. Now there were only five of them left. The two-legged one came up beside them. He pulled the big male close to him and then sent the other four after the man who ran toward the barn.

Raider heard them coming. His leg suddenly didn't hurt anymore. He ran toward the darkness of the stable. The horses were spooking inside. They knew something was wrong. Raider flew through the stable, opening the barn door at the opposite end of the row of stalls. He freed the horses, running them toward the open door. They gladly ran away from the scent of the wolf pack which was in the air. When the last horse had cleared the stable, Raider closed the door and latched it.

He turned in time to see the four shapes entering the barn. They hesitated for a moment and then came straight toward him. But Raider had a plan. He jumped onto a stall and climbed toward the loft.

One of the creatures leaped after him, but Raider managed to swing into the loft ahead of the flashing teeth. He took a deep breath when he was safely in the loft. They wouldn't be able to get to him unless one of them could climb a ladder. He could hear them below, sniffing and whining. He hoped like hell that the two-legged one would come, too.

Raider stood up. He peered toward the front of the stable, where the door was still open. It might work. He'd have to lay the seeds. Using his feet, he began to kick the stale hay from the loft. There were also a couple of bales that had not been tapped. He broke them open and kicked the straw toward the bewildered animals. They whined beneath him. His scent drove them crazy as they searched for a way up. He kept kicking the straw on them. Fire. That would do it. Get them locked in and torch it off.

He peered toward the upper loft door, where the hay bales were loaded and unloaded in the barn. But the loft door was in the rear. How would he get them to stay below? His scent. They followed his scent. He started to take off his shirt. He would hang it on the edge of the loft. They could smell him then.

When the shirt was in place, Raider ran to the loft door. He grabbed the rope and hung there for a second. He had to set the fire off. Drawing his Colt, he sent a flaming burst into the dry straw. A small circle of smoke started to rise.

As he dropped from the loft, he wondered if the wolves had smelled the smoke yet or if the gunfire had scared them away.

When he hit the ground, he tore around the side of the barn, making for the open door. The animals were holding on the scent of his shirt, at least until the doors started to swing shut. He saw them coming. He heard their breathing. They bounced off the door as he slammed it shut. His weight held the door while he fumbled with the latch. It took him a moment, but he finally heard the click as the latch fell into place. Raider stepped back away from his handiwork. He watched as the animals rattled the door, trying to get out. Smoke curled from the loft. Flames began to lick at the roof.

If Raider's leg hadn't been throbbing, he might have felt sorry for them but as it stood, he just turned and walked away from the blaze, leaving the Wolfbrand's children to their deserved fate.

As he headed toward the house, Raider tried to stay low. There was no need to assume that all the animals were dead. Maybe one or two of them had been held back by their master.

He froze in his tracks. The two-legged one had to be around somewhere. Unless he had been imagined. No, Black Dog was their master. His sister had said as much.

He hurried as fast as his wounded leg would let him. The oil lamp still burned in the kitchen. When he entered from the back door, he called to Chaney and the girl. There was no reply. What if Black Dog had found them in the attic?

Raider picked up the oil lamp and started through the kitchen. At the entrance of the parlor, he called again. This time the attic door opened and the ladder came down. Yellow Fox climbed down first. Chaney was slower with his descent.

The old man frowned at Raider. "Well?"

He pointed toward the stable. "I caught four of 'em in a fire. Had to torch your barn."

Chaney waved him off. "I don't care. Are there any left?"

Raider started to say something when he noticed that the girl's eyes had grown wide again.

She was gazing at something over his shoulder.

As he turned, Raider heard the rattling of a rifle lever.

A low growling also filled the air.

Chaney stepped back, holding his chest. "My God."

The two-legged creature stepped out of the shadows. He had the big male next to him, saving him for last. He had known that the big Pinkerton would be hard to kill but now the tide had turned in favor of the Wolfbrand.

"No!" Yellow Fox cried.

Raider scowled at the pointed snout. He wasn't afraid of the hairy face. Not anymore. The big male wolf still had him concerned. So did the rifle.

Black Dog held Raider's own Winchester in his hands. He had found the rifle when he sneaked into the house. Raider knew a wolf wouldn't be able to shoot a rifle. The claws were gone, replaced by human hands.

A voice came out of the snout. "Drop the gun, Pinkerton."

Raider let his Colt fall to the floor. "Hello, Black Dog. I wish I could say I'm glad t' meet you."

The big male wolf growled at him.

"Not yet," Black Dog said, "but you will die, Pinkerton."

Raider had a strange smile on his lips. "Come on, Black Dog. Show us how you change into a man. Do it for me, afore I die."

Raider was hoping to get a chance when the mask came off but Black Dog was too quick. The wolf mask hit the floor beside the Colt and suddenly, the Wolfbrand had become a man.

CHAPTER TWENTY-ONE

Raider stared at the renegade Apache. ''Damned smart, Black Dog. Makin' ever'one think you're a wolf.''

Black Dog did not smile at the big man. ''You must die.''

Yellow Fox moved toward her brother. ''Please—''

Black Dog scowled at her. ''Shut up, sister! You live with the white men. You are like them.''

Raider wondered if the renegade had heard the remark about the burning barn. He had to stall him, to keep him from going after the rest of his pack.

''Took me a while t' figger how you trained them animals,'' Raider said. ''But it come t' me, after I remembered it in a dream.''

The Apache turned his hateful eyes on Raider. ''No. You lie!''

Raider put his arm around Yellow Fox. ''Your brother done trained 'em from pups, honey. Probably got 'em 'fore they opened their eyes. I bet that mask is made from the skin o' their momma.''

The girl nodded. "He told me the same thing when I was in the cave with him and the wolves."

Black Dog's expression did not change. "You killed my children."

Raider started to reply, but Chaney suddenly pushed past him.

The old man glared at the Apache buck. "Why did you kill my family? Tell me? Why did you send those godforsaken creatures after us?"

Yellow Fox put her hand on the old man's shoulder. "No. You don't want to know. My brother is crazy."

Black Dog laughed, proving correct his sister's assessment. "You!" The renengade pointed at Chaney. "Our mother scrubbed your clothes," the renegade said through clenched teeth. "She mopped your floors."

Chaney's eyes grew wide. "No! It can't be!"

"Remember the Indian boy who waited at the edge of your property?" Black Dog cried. "The boy your father didn't want in his house?"

Yellow Fox glared at her kin. "No, brother. No more."

But the Apache madman had no intention of quitting. "Your father sent my mother away because he found you on top of her, Jubal Chaney. She had to go back to her people and bear a half-breed child."

Chaney wheeled to look at Yellow Fox. "You?"

The girl burst into tears.

Chaney staggered backward, falling into a chair.

Raider scowled at Black Dog. "I don't get it, Injun. Why'd you have t' kill Chaney's family? If Yellow Fox is his bastard daughter, you coulda come to him an' told him. You didn't have t' kill 'em."

"Ha!" the renegade cried. "I killed them so he would have to take her in. She is the only family he has now."

Chaney wiped the sweat from his forehead.

Raider looked at the old man. "Is he tellin' the truth?"

Chaney nodded. "I did what he said with the Apache woman. I married rather late. I—my God, why did he have to kill them all? I would have given this girl whatever she wanted. My God, that was twenty years ago. Why do I have to pay for it now?"

The big male wolf growled at Chaney.

Black Dog spoke something in Apache.

The animal stopped growling.

"Trained," Raider said. "An' you put on the mask t' make people think a man could turn into a wolf."

Keep stalling. Find an opening. Maybe the girl would be of some help.

"Ain't no such thing as a man-wolf," Raider went on. "No Apache magic is that strong."

Black Dog grunted, glaring at his sister. "Move!"

Raider saw it coming. The end. He had to try something quickly, even if he had little chance of taking the Indian and the wolf.

Yellow Fox refused to obey her half brother. "I can't let you kill them, Black Dog. They both helped me."

Raider held her close to him. "Do it, Black Dog. You better finish us. Four of your doggies are burnin' in the barn."

The Indian flinched. He cursed in his native tongue. He told his sister to move again. Yellow Fox refused to budge.

"You'll have to kill me, too," she cried.

Black Dog's lip curled. "Sister!"

"No, Black Dog. No!"

The Indian spoke Apache to the big wolf.

As soon as the words had left his mouth, the animal tensed and then sprang straight at Raider.

Without thinking, the big man extended his hands. He caught the animal by the throat as it leaped. The weight of the wolf carried him backward. He hung on, trying to crush the animal's throat.

Black Dog pointed the rifle.

Raider felt the blood gushing between his fingers. The fangs were almost touching his face. Keep a steady hold. Don't give in to the son of a bitch.

The animal yelped. Its body relaxed, going limp.

Black Dog realized he had made a mistake. His finger tightened on the trigger but before he could squeeze off a round from the Winchester, Raider launched the dead wolf in Black Dog's direction.

The Indian had to move to dodge the animal's body.

Raider jumped behind the carcass. He caught the barrel of the rifle, turning it toward the ceiling.

Black Dog tripped the trigger. A slug slammed into the ceiling.

Raider swung his boot, driving a foot into Black Dog's groin.

As the Indian fell, Raider felt the fire in his hands. The barrel of the rifle was still hot. He led go, as did the renegade. The Winchester fell onto the floor.

Raider dived on top of Black Dog. They began to wrestle, rolling back and forth.

Yellow Fox moved toward the rifle, picking it up from the floor.

Black Dog glared at his sister, peering over Raider's shoulder. "Shoot him, Yellow Fox!"

Chaney gawked at the girl. "No!"

Raider heard the lever chortling. She was going to shoot him. She would never side against her brother, not in a matter of life and death.

"Get her, Chaney!" Raider cried.

"Kill him, sister!"

The girl took aim.

Raider looked into the renegade's red face, wondering if it would be last sight he would ever see. He closed his eyes. The rifle exploded. Raider felt Black Dog's body go limp. When he opened his eyes, he saw the hole in the renegade's forehead. Yellow Fox had been an inch shy of hitting him between the eyes. Raider rolled away from the twitching body. He jumped to his feet and gaped at the Apache woman.

Yellow Fox held the rifle on Raider for a moment.

"No!" Chaney cried. "Don't. I'll take you in. You can have anything you want."

She dropped the Winchester to the floor.

Raider limped toward the girl. He held out his arms. Yellow Fox put her face against his chest, crying.

They were motionless until they saw the light from the flames on the roof of the burning barn.

Sheriff Bit Daniels tipped back his hat. He had been staring at the charred remains of the stable. Chaney had gone for the lawman while Raider stayed with Yellow Fox. It had taken a whole day for Daniels to get there.

Raider stepped up next to the lawman. "I know it sounds loco, sheriff, but it happened just like I said."

Daniels chortled. "Let me see if I got this straight. The girl is Chaney's half-breed daughter by the family's old scrubwoman. And Black Dog was tryin' to get even with Chaney for the daughter he didn't even know about. Trained a bunch of wolves. Then come after Chaney."

Raider exhaled. "I know it's farfetched—"

"Naw! Hear about stuff like this every day."

The big man gestured back toward the house. "Look at the girl's eyes. White flecks, just like the old man."

The sheriff sighed. "Well, you got the body of Black Dog, who was s'posed to be dead."

"Probably faked his own death so he could operate. Musta took him years to train them animals. Reckon you should be glad he never made it into Odessa."

That seemed to send a shudder through the lawman's shoulders. Daniels looked back toward the house. "Chaney backed you up on all this. He got his due."

Raider wasn't so sure. "Black Dog tormented him for somethin' I done a lot. I bedded women in my time, a few squaws. But I never suffered for it like that."

Daniels returned to the barn. "Trapped 'em in there, huh? That was pretty smart. Think there's any more of 'em in those mountains?"

"Wolves? I doubt it. And if there are any more, they won't be dangerous; not without their master."

The sheriff shook his head. "I reckon I got to believe you, Raider. But hell, you did break out of my jail."

"I saved your bacon," the big man replied. "You never woulda got reelected if the Wolfbrand had run amok in your town."

Daniels cleared his throat. "Well, that'll never happen now. I'm gonna take Black Dog back for the Indian agent. Have to take the body of that wolf too. And these others that you spread around. Won't have much left of those ones that got burned."

Raider knew the lawman would take credit for stopping Black Dog. But the big man didn't care. As long as he was free, the sheriff could do whatever he wanted. The case was just another report for the Pinkerton files.

"I need a ride back t' town," Raider told the sheriff.

Daniels nodded. "Soon as I get it all on the wagon."

Raider turned and started back toward the house.

"Hey," Daniels called, "ain't you gonna help me?"

Raider laughed. "Shit no. I killed 'em, you load 'em up."

No need to tell the lawman that the girl had actually pulled the trigger on her brother.

He stepped up onto the back porch. "Anybody home?"

Chaney and Yellow Fox were sitting at the kitchen table.

The big man stood in the door, looking at their tired faces. "Well, it's over. Or is it?"

Chaney glanced at the girl. "I want her to stay with me. Black Dog was right about one thing. She's the only kin I have now. And she didn't know what he was doing."

Raider nodded. "That's right Christian of you, Chaney. You gonna stay with him, Yellow Fox?"

She hesitated and then replied: "For now."

Raider felt sort of sad. "Anythin' I can do for you, Chaney?"

The old merchant lifted his white-ringed eyes. "You've done all that I've asked of you, Raider. I can't expect any more."

An awkward silence fell over them.

Raider wanted to say good-bye but somehow the words wouldn't come, so he just turned and left them there at the table. Maybe it wouldn't hurt to help the sheriff a little. He didn't want any trouble for a while. He just wanted to kick back, free and easy.

At least until he got the telegram from William Wagner.

CHAPTER TWENTY-TWO

William Wagner cried out when he opened the telegraph message. "Oh, my God. No!"

The other clerks working in the office stopped at their tasks, looking toward the desk of their boss.

Wagner waved them back to their work. "I'm not paying you to gawk and goldbrick!" The second-in-command of the agency felt badly about his chiding remark, but the gravity of the communiqué had thrown him off. He should have known it was bad news as soon as he saw the telegraph operator leaving the office in a hurry. There was nothing to do but inform Allan Pinkerton of the turn of events in Carson City. Another agent was in trouble. Only this time it was a matter of life and death.

A knock on Pinkerton's door evoked a quarrelsome burst from the burly Scotsman. "Another fury comes to plague me! Who's there?"

Wagner opened the door. "You probably don't want to hear this, but Henry Stokes is still in trouble."

Pinkerton scowled at his ramrod. "I knew we shouldn't have sent him to Nevada. What did he do this time?"

Wagner figured it was best to blurt it out. "The powers that be intend to hang him next month."

Pinkerton made a disgusted noise. "Have they at least given him a fair trial? My God, he deserves that."

"According to this, there has been a trial," Wagner replied, "but I doubt that it was a fair one. Henry has been railroaded."

Pinkerton stood up, starting to pace behind his desk. "Isn't it always the way? Our men try to find the truth and the locals won't let them. My God, what are we going to do?"

Wagner exhaled, removing his wire-rimmed glasses for a methodical cleaning. "In Nevada, the government is still a territorial seat. That means the powers that be are pretty much the reigning judges and marshals. If Stokes got the wrong judge, his guilt or innocence wouldn't matter."

Pinkerton rubbed his thick beard. "Well, we both know what this means. We have to spring him. Can we do it legally?"

Wagner shook his head. "I doubt it. Drat, why didn't he leave when they let him out on bail?"

"Stokes is like a snapping turtle. Once he grabs something, he won't let go. He's a good man."

Wagner refrained from pointing out that Pinkerton had been cursing the agent's name only a few weeks before.

"All right," the big Scotsman said finally. "Spring him. Send somebody who can get the job done."

"I heard from Raider yesterday," Wagner replied. "He wrapped up the case in west Texas. Something about a renegade Apache and a pack of wolves. He's ready to go again."

"Send him to Nevada immediately."

Wagner nodded.

"And William!"

"Yes?"

"Tell Raider to make sure they both get out alive."

Wagner closed the office door behind him. He knew if anybody could spring Henry Stokes, it was surely the big man from Arkansas. Of course, the fates would decide if they both got out alive. Wagner just wondered if providence would be tolerant of Raider's blazing six-gun.

As it happened, however, the big man never had to fire a shot.

CHAPTER TWENTY-THREE

Hangings, like rodeos and picnics, carried a certain social expectation west of the Mississippi. People came from miles around, from neighboring territories, to watch an outlaw swing from the end of a rope. Territorial law enforcement officials viewed the spectacle as a chance to show evildoers what fate awaited them if they erred within the borders of the realm.

Henry Stokes sat in his cell, listening as the hangman tested the trapdoor on the gallows that was meant for him. Stokes didn't care about the local officials. He had been railroaded, of course, but that was no longer the issue. Nor was the fact of his innocence very important to the stocky Pinkerton agent. Henry wanted to be freed, and on this particular morning, set for his execution, he didn't care how his liberation came.

He had refused a last meal, figuring that one of his brethren, at the insistence of the agency, would free him in the end. Of course, it probably wouldn't be that sniveling kid they sent to get the lawyer. Wagner would send Hartman or Avery; maybe even Raider if the big galoot was free.

Sweat poured off the agent's forehead. Wagner was cutting it awfully close but surely he wouldn't let Stokes die. Henry had done little more than discover the truth about one of the local rich men. They had framed him for it and now he was going to take that last walk.

The door opened to the cell room. Stokes looked over, thinking that someone had come with his reprieve. Instead, the dapper, fool-faced marshal entered with two of his deputies. "Time to go, Henry."

"You don't have to smile so much."

"I ain't the one who's dyin'," the marshal replied.

The key turned in the cell door.

"Since I didn't get a last meal, how 'bout one more request?" Stokes asked.

The marhsal frowned. "What might that be?"

"Don't hang me."

A laugh from the lawman. "You are a stitch, Henry. I'm gonna miss you bein' in my jail."

Henry couldn't say the same thing. He stood up. "Well, let's get it over with."

The marshal frowned again. "Seems a shame to hang a man with such a good sense of humor."

"Imagine how it looks from my end," Stokes replied.

They led him out of the marshal's office.

The crowd cheered when the condemned man walked toward the gallows.

Henry could not really blame them for being excited. Many times he had taken his own satisfaction from seeing guilty men swing. Of course, Henry was innocent but they had no way of knowing that.

His eyes scanned the crowd, looking for his liberator. Where the hell was Hartman or Avery? He would have given anything to see Raider staring at him with those balck eyes. He passed the lawyer who had presided over his case.

"I'm sorry, Mr. Stokes," the book thumper said.

Stokes just shook his head. He couldn't blame the inept attorney for the partial jury and the hanging judge. Why the hell hadn't he taken it on the lam when he got out on bail the first time? He had to stay and do his job. Damn it all, why had he ever come back to work for Pinkerton?

The stairs were steep leading up to the gallows. Both deputies held his arms as he climbed. It was hard to ascend with his hands tied behind him. This was it. There would be no reprieve this time.

The hangman waited with a black hood over his head.

Stokes looked at the marshal. "How come he's wearin' that hood?"

"Because he volunteered for the job," the lawman replied. "Doesn't want the rest of the community to know who he is. Can't say as I blame him. Would you want to have a drink with a hangman?"

"I would if it meant he wasn't hangin' me," Stokes replied.

The marshal shook his head. "Sure gonna miss you, Henry."

Stokes sighed, looking out over the crowd. "Yeah, I bet you are."

"Any last words?" the marshal asked.

Stokes said that he wasn't in a talkative mood.

The marshal nodded to the hangman.

A strong hand grabbed Henry and pulled him toward the rope. He felt the trap door beneath his feet. "Put the knot on the side," Stokes told him.

"Do what I say, Henry, and there won't be no hangin'." The familiar voice startled Stokes.

"Rai—"

He felt a fist in his back, shutting off his wind.

The hangman motioned for the marshal to climb down from the gallows.

Stokes caught a glimpse of the eyes inside the mask. Two black irises peered out at him from the eyeholes. How the hell was Raider going to save him in the big crowd? It didn't matter. The big man from Arkansas was there, masquerading as the hangman.

What happened next stunned the crowd, as well as the law enforcement officials of the territory of Nevada.

• • •

William Wagner stared at the letter that had fallen on his desk. It had come in from Henry Stokes. Wagner knew that Raider had saved Stokes from the gallows, but now the official report was there.

He opened it and began to read the scrawled writing.

"Well, Wagner, you did right. Raider was there, pretending to be the hangman. Volunteered for the job. Nobody knew who he was. So when the trap door opened, Raider grabbed me and jumped off the gallows. We hit the dirt hard but I didn't care cause I was alive."

Wagner sighed. He had already received word from the territorial government of Nevada. The governor had condemned the actions of the Pinkerton agency, saying that their operatives would no longer be welcome in Nevada. He decided to read on.

"So there we were in the middle of the crowd, Wagner. Raider still had on the hangman's hood. People seemed to get out of our way pretty good. Raider had it all figured. Didn't tie the rope too well, so it came loose. I still had it around my neck when we jumped on the horse.

"Well, they shot at us, but everybody was surprised, so they missed pretty good. We rode the hell out of town and kept going till we got to the California border. A posse followed us for a while, but we threw them off. Raider left me in Stockton to catch the train. I asked to stay with him, but you know how he is. That's the way it happened, Wagner. Honest to God. Let me tell you, I'm glad to be away from Nevada. And I ain't never going back there for no reason. But you can send me where you like cause I'm ready to work again."

Wagner was nodding appreciatively when Allan Pinkerton moved in front of his desk. "You seem pleased, William."

He held up the letter. "The official word on the incident with Stokes in Nevada."

"I won't rest until our name is cleared!" Pinkerton cried. "Do you hear me?"

"We'll just have to do what we can, sir."

"See that you do. By the way, where are Raider and Henry?"

Wagner shrugged. "Raider's on a case. I'm about to send Stokes another assignment, if that's all right with you."

Pinkerton didn't have to think about it very long. He told Wagner he had just the case for Stokes. And he had no doubt that there would be an assignment for Raider as soon as the big man had finished his current duty.

EPILOGUE

Dallas was cold and rainy as Raider slopped through the mud. He rode the same black stallion that had been given to him by the man in Odessa—what was his name? Chaney? The man who had been plagued by wolves had presented him with the stallion before he left to go help Henry Stokes. Raider had tried to ride the animal into the ground, but the black was too strong for him.

It had been months since Raider left Odessa. Now, on a drizzling February day, he was back in Texas, delivering a prisoner to the marshal in Dallas. It was the prisoner who attracted all the attention during Raider's muddy trek up Main Street. Not because the outlaw was alive, but because he was slung belly-down on the saddle of the horse that trailed the big man's black stallion.

Gawkers lined the sidewalk, even in the rain. Curtains in windows parted so wives and children could have a look at the terrible sight. But it wasn't horrible enough to make them turn away. It was something to relish, to gossip about, to remember in the coming years.

Raider reined up in front of the marshal's office.

The lawman came out to greet him. "Dead, huh?"

Raider wasn't in the mood for games. "Don't nothin' get by you, marshal."

"Did you have to kill him?" the lawman asked.

Raider shrugged. "No. But if I hadn'ta killed him, he probably woulda killed me."

A sigh from the marshal. "Well, it don't matter. Save the state of Texas the price of a hangin'."

Raider handed him the reins of the dead man's horse. "I'll be glad to sign any papers you got."

"Maybe later," the lawman replied. "Where'd you catch him?"

"Near the Oklahoma border. Had a lot of snow up that way so he had to stop to rest."

"How'd you get him?"

"I never stopped," Raider said. "Look here, I'll jaw with you later. I gotta get warm."

The marshal gestured toward his office. "You can wait by my potbellied stove while I get the undertaker."

Raider shook his head. "That ain't what I had in mind."

"I see." A smile stretched over the marshal's mouth. "You're goin' to see Margie again. Ain't you?"

Raider just took the reins of his own mount and started for the livery. The stallion deserved to be treated like a rich man's pony. It was one of the best damned animals that the big man had ever ridden.

"Say hello to Margie for me," the marshal called.

Raider just walked on, a surly figure in the rain.

People pointed at him, whispering as he passed but it didn't matter to Raider what they said. A mountain lion never worried about a pack rat.

He stabled the stallion and then headed for the woman's place.

Margie Worth had been a whore until Dallas got too respectable to accept her. She opted to become a cook after that. Margie had never taken much to having men around full-time. But she always opened her door for Raider.

"Lordy, Ray, you look like somethin' that was swallowed by a wolf and shit off a cliff."

The big man smiled. "Aw, I ain't that bad, am I?"

"You won't be when I get finished with you."

Margie gave him the royal treatment. Bath, shave, haircut, whiskey, food. Raider was trying to grab her after he was clean.

"Not yet," Margie told him. "I got somethin' for you."

Raider chuckled. "Yeah, and it's right between your legs."

"Oh, you'll get that soon enough," she replied. "But this is somethin' else again."

She crossed the room to rummage through a chest of drawers.

Raider watched her backside. "Margie, how come you ain't got fat now that you're cookin'? Most cooks get fat."

"Oh, I reckon 'cause I don't like food any better'n I used to like men."

She turned with an envelope in her hand. "Listen, a boy was through here about two weeks ago lookin' for you. Said his name was Stokes."

"Henry? What'd he have t' say?"

She tapped the letter with the back of her hand. "Well, he said that business in Nevada has been cleared up. Said they hung the right man. You Pinks can work in Nevada now."

Raider shrugged. "Big deal. I hate Nevada. What the hell is that letter about?"

"Well, that Henry left it for you at the marshal's office, but the marshal told him to bring it here."

Raider smiled a little, looking over at Margie's bed. "What's it say?"

She frowned at him. "What makes you think I read it?"

"Margie, I know you. You read it a hundred times since you got it."

She sighed but then nodded. "Okay, I read it. Are you mad?"

"No, just tell me what it says, that way I won't have t' read it myself."

She urged him toward the bed and then sat down next to him. "It came from a man name of Chaney."

"Really? The man from Odessa?"

"That's him," Margie rejoined. "Said to tell you that things are better now. He's got that girl livin' with him. Treatin' her just like a daughter. Said he hoped you get the letter 'cause he sent it to the agency. Look here, posted five months ago."

"Hmm. Reckon I was lucky t' get it. Right now I'd feel lucky if I got somethin' else."

He slid his arm around her waist.

Margie shrugged away. "I ain't finished yet."

Raider sighed. "Okay, what's the rest?"

"Well, he says that girl, Yellow Fox, is expectin' a baby. Seems she took up with the livery man there in Odessa. And Chaney says he's happy about it all. Says if he can't get his family back, at least he has the girl and the baby. Also says that his business is good and he plans to take the livery man in as his partner."

Raider put his hands behind his head. "What else?"

Margie looked into his eyes. "That's it."

"You sure?"

She pulled her gown over her head, revealing her firm body. "Nothin' more. Here, let me get you started." She reached under the towel that had been wrapped around his waist. Her touch felt good on his cock. He sprang to life.

Margie slipped down next to him. She guided his hand to her own crotch. "Now, you touch me." Her cunt was as wet as the weather.

It didn't take him long to roll over and enter her.

When they were finished, Margie climbed off the bed. "Oh, ain't it grand when things work out all for the best."

But he never heard her. The big man had closed his eyes, praying for dreamless slumber as he gradually began to slip away.